Savage Realms Monthly: March 2025

A collection of dark fantasy sword and sorcery adventures

Carl Walmsey, Tim Gerstmar, Grayson Sullivan

Literary Rebel, LLC

SAVAGE REALMS
MONTHLY

TALES OF SWORDS AND SORCERY

Copyright © 2025 by Literary Rebel, LLC

All rights reserved.

No part of this publication may be reproduced, distributed, or transmitted in any form or by any means, including photocopying, recording, or other electronic or mechanical methods, without the prior written permission of the publisher, except as permitted by U.S. copyright law. For permission requests, contact www.literaryrebel.com

The story, all names, characters, and incidents portrayed in this production are fictitious. No identification with actual persons (living or deceased), places, buildings, and products is intended or should be inferred.

1st edition March 2025

Contents

From the Desk of the Editor	VIII
Interested in advertising with us?	IX
1. In the Jungles of the Thing God	1
Meet the Author	27
Discover the Savage Realms Game Books	30
2. Cursed	32
Meet the Author	65
Variant Cover B	68
3. The Voice in the Mist	69
Meet the Author	88
Art Exclusive - Fan Service	91
Free Book Offer	92
Interested in advertising with us?	94
Submissions	95
Afterword	96

COLLECT ALL YOUR FAVORITE ISSUES

SAVAGE REALMS MONTHLY: MARCH 2025

Miss an issue? Grab all your favorite sword and sorcery fiction: bit.ly/SavageMag

From the Desk of the Editor

by William Miller

If this is your first time picking up a copy of the Savage Realms, let me welcome to the future of sword and sorcery fiction! This is the monthly publication that aims to revitalize the sword and sorcery genre with talented new authors telling tales of high adventure. We work hard every month to bring you the best in short fantasy fiction by emerging authors. Last month marked our 100th story published. This month, we've got our sights set on 100 more! We hope you'll join us for the journey.

So without further ado...

Interested in advertising with us?

Have you published a fantasy or science fiction book? Are you struggling to get sales? Would you'd like to reach potentially thousands of new readers?

Place an advertisement with Savage Realms Monthly!

We've got a dedicated fan base eager to find new and exciting books by talented authors.

Reach out to us: https://www.literaryrebel.com/contact/ to discuss ad options.

In the Jungles of the Thing God

by Tim Gerstmar

Flinty-eyed horsemen watched them from the grassy banks of the Zanish coast. Rosnick, a young, battle-tested runaway gazed back from the forward lookout position on the *Alizarin Witch*. Fierce winds whipped the horsemen's cloaks about like great wings of dark angels, and their horned helms glittered in the tropical sunlight. They were foreign specters or dreams, food for anecdotal sea stories.

Tall, lean-muscled Jagen, pirate captain of the *Alizarin Witch*, stepped onto the weather decks.

"The Zanish people are superstitious, Rosnick. You shouldn't stare too long. They cast evil curses with a glance. You'll lose your memory and never leave."

"And what do you believe?" said Rosnick, forcing a laugh.

"I believe in strong mead and the warm body of a willing harlot, aye, Uplander? I reckon we'll find that soon enough in Yanir. Don't expect a big city like Krell. But you'll enjoy it. They have their own wild ways there. We'll toast to our victory and your swift sword arm."

Jagen clapped Rosnick on his muscled back, which was deeply bronzed from many leagues at the oars. The horsemen cantered along, following the Witch a way before turning their mounts inland toward the orange light of the setting sun, as the Witch moved into the palm-lined mouth of the Nag River. The crew sang a vain death dirge, half daring the gods to make them die young and valorous.

Yanir was built on stilts in the Nag Delta. Warm light glowed from the oil lamps in the floating mead halls, and the crew of the *Alizarin Witch* hoisted their flagons to the various gods of their peoples. There were plenty of buxom maidens seeking partners for the night to soothe bad memories.

Rosnick brooded quietly, as was his wont when glutted with mead. The bar banter became dim and fuzzy as he slipped into a shallow sleep. He started up as a pale slip of a vixen sat across from him. She wore leather armor tailored to breathe in the hot climate, and her face was framed by silky, black hair, like a war mane. The teeth of a great river serpent jangled about her ivory neck on a leather cord.

"What do you want, wench?" said Rosnick.

"I am Zanzar. Not a wench," she said, leaning forward. "Tell me your name. I never drink with strangers."

"Rosnick of Upland."

"An Uplander. You say that with a fair deal of pride. I thought your people feared the wicked world. You're brave, aren't you? A brave Uplander."

"If you're not a bar wench, what are you doing here, and why haven't you been raped?"

Zanzar's hand flashed to her hip. Rosnick reached for the pommel of his sword, but drink slowed his reflexes, and he froze as he felt the cold edge of a cutlass against his throat. Zanzar's eyes sparkled with mischief. Rosnick relaxed back into his seat and withdrew his hand from the pommel of his weapon.

"I'm here with my crew," she said, gesturing to a ring of raucous Karkunmen at a far table, their chins wet with mead, foreign songs falling from their lips like the tinkling of bamboo flutes.

"A captain," said Rosnick.

"Does that surprise you?"

Zanzar sat back and smiled, sad and white, like she wanted the night to go on for eternity. Rosnick looked drunkenly out into the darkness of the jungle and the glassy river that wound through it.

"And tonight?" said Rosnick.

"A bit of this," said Zanzar, producing an ivory pipe with a long stem.

"What is it?"

"Yanish weed. The finest. Care to try?"

Rosnick remembered standing on rubbery legs, the room spinning. The strange vibrations of the mead hall pulsed with his robust blood flow. Then he was soaring across the earth, fast over vast plains and plateaus covered with crumbling cities. In the distance was a singular, black, onion-domed tower overlooking the sea. He floated toward it, hovering over the land like a passenger bird, and Zanzar's voice was there.

See far. See the river and the old city. See.

He awoke amidst a heap of furs, the smell of impassioned love hanging in the air. He rubbed his brow, recalling latter fragments of the strange dream when it turned sour and there appeared before him a disembodied head with diamond eyes that burned with savage fire. His stomach churned with the side-to-side listing of a swift ship. This was not the *Alizarin Witch*. Rosnick sought his garments and his weapon, dressed, and stumbled onto the deck, his stomach threatening to unleash its contents. A crew of sun-bronzed Karkunmen worked the rigging and pulled at oars with vein-popping, muscular arms. Some scrubbed the immaculate deck. All around them was the chorus of jungle life with its untraceable multitude of voices. Zanzar perched above him on the rigging.

"Good morning, Uplander. Welcome to the *Hell Cat*."

"How did I get here?" said Rosnick.

"Don't think so much. This is the way of things," replied Zanzar. "It's the way of the sea."

"I want an answer."

"You signed on."

"I did?"

"Ah yes, the Yanish weed. It makes you do odd things. In some ways, more truthful things than we would do otherwise. They say it opens the doors to the heart. Do you feel as though you've opened your heart?"

Rosnick laughed.

"Don't concern yourself too much, Rosnick. You have agreed to a significant share of the lay. I made sure of it. And you've joined with a fierce bunch. We are the reavers of the great Nag. We have nothing to fear. For we are fear."

The Karkunmen screamed a hearty huzzah, and the prow of the sleek vessel plied its way into the darkness of the imposing jungle. Zanzar swung down from the rigging with the strength of a lioness. She stood before Rosnick and yelled to the Karkunmen in a voice plated with bronze. A rangy Karkunman with heavily muscled shoulders, head shaven along the sides and a look of shrewd practicality, reported.

"Rosnick, this is my first mate, Keeve."

Keeve nodded, and he and Rosnick shook hands, the Karkunmen stone-faced.

"I hope you're handy on the deck," said Keeve. "There aren't many boats in Upland."

"I sailed with the *Alizarin Witch*. We clove the skulls of marauding sea wolves off the coast of Kresh."

Keeve ignored Rosnick and looked at Zanzar.

"Rosnick will be assisting me," said Zanzar.

Keeve nodded with a roll of his eyes and then returned to mending a sail.

"Don't mind Keeve," said Zanzar. "He does not trust easily. I feel you're quite similar, Rosnick."

Rosnick and Zanzar looked into each other's eyes, and for a moment she again appeared wistful.

"Do you trust me?" she said.

"I suppose."

"I have something to tell you, Rosnick. I have seen a city in my dreams. I know it may be the madness of the Yanish herbs, but it felt so real, so solid. Have you seen such a thing?"

He did not answer.

"No need to tell me, Rosnick. I feel you have, as well. They say the weed of the Yanish coast opens a window into forgotten worlds."

"It's nothing but a drug vision," he said. "A dream. There is nothing real about it. Dreams are only a reflection of our thoughts and visions, nothing more."

"And what good is the world without them?"

"What good is a world without things that I can see and touch, and taste? Dreams have no flavor. I laugh at them. Give me what is real."

"Keeve, man the rigging! I'm going below for a bit. Come Rosnick."

She took him by the hand and led him to her stateroom.

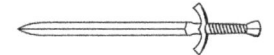

Several days later the *Hell Cat* was beyond the Uradu Forests, far into the savage territory of shadowy tigers and mighty river serpents. There was the occasional shifting and rustling in the mangroves, and the dark creep of grey shapes passing by. Once, Rosnick saw faces watching them, like the haunted members of a dying race that had never heard the common tongue. At night, while on watch, the coppery eyes of black leopards flickered from the branches of trees like the rounded wings of iridescent moths.

That night, when Rosnick ended his watch, he returned to the furs and the Yanish weed in Zanzar's cabin. She tested even his virulent, young lust. There was a curious familiarity to her company, as if her very touch activated a forgotten part of himself. The weed imbued the passion with strength and tragedy, giving the lovemaking a kind of magnificence. Once asleep he dreamt of the most vivid phantasmagorical journeys. In one, he was in a grand, lustrous city. A hand reached up—his own hand—and a great bird alighted upon the gleaming, golden bracer on his forearm. With his other hand he reached out to a young woman with silky, black hair and eyes like opal moons. Her lips were full and wide. And she spoke to him, in Zanzar's voice.

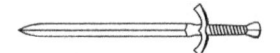

He could only ever recall fragments from the dreams, and these became distant and hazy as the day began, and the two lovers never spoke of them.

On the third day, Zanzar suggested him to lead the oarsmen for an hour or two, which he did. Later he taught some of the Karkunmen the basics of Upland swordsmanship. All listened eagerly, save Keeve.

"Your feints and parries are for the steppes and the open plain, Rosnick. They will not serve on the rough seas."

"Is that what you'd call this river?" said Rosnick. "A rough sea?"

"I'd call it miserable and stinking."

"Care to go a round?" said Rosnick, twirling one of the wooden training swords about.

Keeve laughed, and in the midst of Rosnick's display, stepped in and pushed the youngster down. Rosnick fell with a clatter, to which the crew responded with uproarious laughter.

Keeve reached out a heavy, brown hand, his smile wide and toothy.

"Come on, Rosnick. You have skill, but we Karkunmen spend life from day one on the sea. Admittedly, your swordplay may work on a slack, mosquito-infested river like this."

Rosnick took the Karkunman's hand and started to rise off the deck. He paused, nodded his thanks to Keeve, and just before he was fully up, he grabbed Keeve's wrist with both hands and fell back with all his weight, launching the startled Keeve over him and across the deck.

Rosnick stood, laughing. The crew joined in.

"Idiots! Quit clowning. Ahead!" yelled Zanzar from her nest in the rigging. "Just up beyond the black water."

Zanzar ordered the ship to draw up close to the muddy shore where the waters were as still as a dead man's blood. A stone totem jutted from the mud close to the water line. The Karkunmen gossiped in quiet tones, gesturing to the primordial effigy.

"This is it," said Zanzar.

"What?" said Rosnick.

"It's exactly as I pictured it," she said, her eyes held by the statue, which was vaguely man-shaped with large globular eyes.

"The dream?" he said.

"Come, Uplander. This is the place. The ancient city is not far. I'm certain of it," said Zanzar, looking suddenly lively and less mesmerized. "All hands. We go ashore here. We're going inland. Rosnick and I will lead. Heed him well. His commands are my commands."

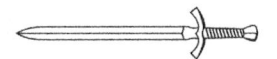

Zanzar, Rosnick, and a detachment of Karkunmen, including Keeve, followed a faint trail that led to a stilt village not all that dissimilar to Yanir, though it was waterlogged and shambling into the muck. The boards creaked beneath their weight, threatening to collapse, and moss hung from the splitting timbers. All was quiet, save the droning chatter of insects and bird life.

A creaking off to the left alerted them, and a man staggered out of one of the buildings, seemingly drunk, though it was difficult to imagine much in the way of liquor here. He was naked, and even from this small distance they could see that his body was covered in tribal scarification.

The Karkunmen muttered hushed prayers, their eyes moving to him warily.

"Take him." Zanzar ordered, shoving several of her crew in the direction of the stranger.

They hesitated, but Keeve nodded, and they moved in on the man, who gave no resistance. They pulled him over to Rosnick and Zanzar. He was young, with the sleek bone structure of the southern tribesmen. His cheeks were covered in the same scarified pattern as his body. He grinned with a mouth full of peg-like teeth.

"Does anyone here speak Southern?" said Rosnick.

"Aye, Captain. I know a bit of South Yan. He may understand," said a stocky Karkunman with close-set eyes.

They spoke in flowing, silky tones. When finished, the Karkunman frowned and shook his head.

"What did he say?" said Zanzar.

"From what I can understand, most of his people have gone inland."

"Then what's he doing here?" said Zanzar.

The Karkunman spoke with the prisoner once more.

"I couldn't catch all of what he said, but he said he was looking for food, that there is little of it where they are."

"Ask him about the city that is supposed to be here."

"He says he can take us there. It's on the way to his people," said the translator.

Eyes wide, the captive glanced about at the Karkunmen sailors as if seeking goodly approval. Finding none, he looked away.

"Rosnick, Keeve. We will go, along with ten others. The rest will remain with the *Hell Cat*," said Zanzar.

Rosnick turned the rope around the captive's neck, leashing him like a hound, and ordering him to lead on. The exotic chant of jungle life trilled and taunted as they grunted their way over muddy, boulder-laden paths that went up and down erratically. Sweat poured from their bodies in salt-depleting rivers. The vines and foliage clung to them like the fingers of a corpse, yet the savage guide moved dexterously and seemed not to sweat.

At the bottom of a long but gradual decline, the forest opened into a ruined city. Great slabs of stone carved with moss-covered battle scenes crisscrossed with massive vines emerging from the muck. The moldering stone visages of ancient gods and forgotten rulers lay in slow entropy, partially buried in their marshy graves, their worn faces demanding recognition of their might. There was a caw, and above them a colorful bird with long tailfeathers circled playfully.

"We'll spread out and see what we can find," ordered Zanzar.

Rosnick and Keeve led their squad to a singularly well-preserved stone archway, the sides of which were illustrated with a crude epic that seemed to involve citizens paying homage to some kind of winged god or goddess. In some of the cartoons, the people were being torn apart by crudely sketched winged beings.

A head was carved above the arch, a man with a skull cap, blank eyes, chiseled jaw, and lips sensitively etched into a cruel grin. Head still foggy from the Yanish weed, Rosnick puzzled over the realistic physiognomy. He stumbled, holding tight to the roped prisoner, who offered an inscrutable smile.

The Karkunmen walked uneasily through the arch, the stone head watching with amusement. The first man pointed to something at their feet and there were murmurs amongst them. There was fresh blood on the stones. The prisoner's eyes were fixed on the blood, which led in a rakish trail to a square pit several paces beyond the arch. The blood trailed off the edge into the pit, as if some wounded creature had crawled or been dragged into it. There was a cryptic sigil painted on the smooth stone floor of the pit, and four large, melted candles were positioned in each corner.

A flapping noise drew their attention back to the arch as something squat and black landed into a crouch above the stone head. It was a dark, hairless monkey, its eyes red and blind. It craned its bald head about on a rubbery neck, as if searching. Its arms were long, and under each were great leathery wings, anatomically like those of a flying squirrel. Its face had a kind of primal intelligence.

The colorful bird's caw echoed through the city, and it swirled low. In seeking a branch on a nearby tree, it happened to pass closely to the ape thing, which began leaping up and down in excited hops, its long arms stretching upward. The slightly translucent, membranous wings glowed with sunlight as it reached up and snatched the bird out of the air. It bit into the poor creature's abdomen, spilling the glistening intestines onto the archway. The thing's teeth were like razors, and it smiled and wiped its bloody maw with the back of its hand after dropping the twitching, uneaten carcass onto the ground at the sailors' feet.

The creature leered and bobbed up and down on its haunches for a moment, baring its teeth in a wicked smile. It raised its long, wiry arms above its head, spreading its blue, vein-lined wings. It opened its mouth, fangs fully extended and so large they were out of proportion to its scholarly head, and it swooped down. It fell upon one of the Karkunmen, knocking him back into the pit. The sailor screamed, and he hit the dusty stone below with a sickening thump. His lower leg was twisted almost perpendicular to his body. He screamed. The monkey thing was upon him, avulsing the flesh on his skull with its awful, yellow canines.

The captive took advantage of the confusion and broke free, but Keeve managed to grab him. The wounded sailor screamed as the creature bit and clawed him multiple times. Its long, rubbery fingers were wrapped about his skull. Rosnick leapt into the pit and rolled to his feet, swinging wide as he came up to cleave the thing's head from its shoulders. The bloody jaws champed spasmodically as it rolled into a corner. The body itself continued to spasm and flop about horribly, the terrible wings slapping and battering the wounded Karkunman in its death convulsions.

Rosnick kicked the body of the bat thing to the side and called for the others to send down a rope. In the shadows of the pit, something glittered in the dark recesses. There was a chittering sound, and shapes moved about cautiously, keeping to the shadows. The Karkunmen's fellows hoisted the wounded man out of the pit and tended to him, bandaging his wounds and wrapping him in a large cloth.

The captive savage laughed. His eyes were wide, saliva running down his chin as he bared his peg-like teeth.

Rosnick stepped forward, and without pause rammed his longsword into the man's gut and out his back. The savage died slowly on the ground.

"Send for Zanzar," said Rosnick to Keeve.

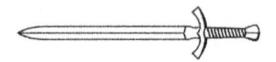

"It's a man," said Rosnick, kicking the body of the creature.

"I've never seen a man like that," said Keeve.

"Look at the shoulders, and the shape of the head."

They turned to the dead captive, who lay with open, staring eyes, mouth frozen in a death grimace.

The wounded Karkunman wailed. Keeve held him and whispered in his ear. A cracking branch drew their attention to the forest around the ruins. Black shapes hovered in the trees. One by one they appeared, alighting on branches. They danced up and down, gnashing their teeth and gesturing to their fellows with obscene waves. Through the trees the grey shapes of men looked out, but they kept to the shadows. The flying apes appeared unconcerned with them.

"To the *Hell Cat*," said Zanzar.

They crossed the dead city completely exposed. The shadows of men paced them ghostly. The pirates plunged through vines and ferns so thick they couldn't see more than three feet in front of them. There was a scream from the rear and the thump of someone falling. Rosnick rushed back to find a Karkunmen sailor lying with an arrow through his side, writhing and wincing as his blood-slick hands pulled in vain at the shaft. Rosnick lifted him, draped his arm over his shoulder and started dragging him toward the ship. A flurry of whistling, like giant hornets, passed close overhead, and then the man screamed one last time as he was struck through the neck with another arrow.

Rosnick let the lifeless body slide to the ground.

The hunkered shapes of two natives appeared in the dappled green light. They raised willowy longbows.

Keeve was by his side with another of the Karkunmen, and the three charged into the assault. Rosnick rushed in low, swinging upward with his longsword, cutting through the bow of the foremost archer and up into his jaw, the arrow flying wildly into the forest. Keeve and his comrade cut down the other, but more arrows sailed through the trees, and the dark shapes of the bat creatures flew in above them. They raced blindly through the thick jungle, toward the *Hell Cat*.

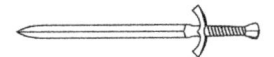

The sails were in ribbons, and the ship was deserted.

"The oars are missing, as well," said Keeve.

The wounded man was laid out on the deck. He shivered and screamed. Zanzar retrieved the pipe and put the stem to his lips. He breathed the heavy smoke of the Yanish weed and was soon quiet, his eyes glassy and staring.

The crew sat around him, exhausted from the day's ordeal. Night approached, and they bathed the injured man and bound his wounds with strips of sail cloth.

"We'll keep a strict watch," said Zanzar. "Tomorrow, at first light, we repair the sails and make some oars."

"Why not now?" said Keeve.

"Because it's dark. We all want out of here. Jaygar, you and Valance have the first watch."

Rosnick followed Zanzar to the bow, where they meditated on the darkening forest.

"Nothing can be done. Tomorrow," she said, putting the pipe between her lips.

"What are you doing?" said Rosnick.

Zanzar held the pipe before her, as if startled that it was suddenly in her hands.

"I told you not to think too much. And not to worry. You're more wench than man, aren't you, Uplander?" she said.

Rosnick batted the pipe out of her hand. Zanzar unsnapped her sheath and drew the cutlass.

"Care to test your strength for real this time, Uplander?"

"It's caused mischief enough," he said, stabbing his finger toward the pipe.

Zanzar shook, lips trembling with fury. She gripped the pommel tighter, face frozen in a snarl. After a few tense moments her muscles relaxed, and she lowered the blade.

"I'm sorry, Rosnick," she said.

She picked up the pipe and inhaled the blissful weed, letting out a great plume of smoke. She offered it to Rosnick. He shook his head.

"You still think you have control, don't you? I've been in far worse situations. We are the crew of the *Hell Cat*, and we do not tremble. Come, you sense it, don't you?"

Zanzar took another puff, and then Rosnick asked for the pipe, succumbing to desperate lovemaking and dreams.

In the dream, he reclined in a marble bath. Across the large, pillared bathing house a bronzed, young girl with raven-black hair approached, stepping lithely across the tiled floor, up the steps and into the steamy water, her brown legs glistening. Upon her ankle was a tattoo of a chain. They spoke, but the dreaming Uplander could not hear the words.

The strange sands of dream shifted, and he was once again with the girl, poring over the pages of an ancient grimoire bound in a murderer's skin. He placed his hand on hers, and they looked into each other's eyes. Their moment was interrupted when a door opened, and five armed guardsmen entered.

His dream-self quarreled with them, ordered them to leave. But they, who at one time obeyed every command he gave, laughed and bound his wrists.

Once again, the dreamscape shifted, and he found himself chained in a stone pit, straining at his bonds as above him black shapes circled and danced, swooping in at him in a sudden rush.

A monstrous yell tore them from dream-haunted slumber. Swords in hand they rushed to a scene of moonlit horror. The two sailors who had been on watch now lay mutilated on the deck, the wounded man standing above their prostrate forms, eyes cold and pinpoint, hunched like some wild beast. Blood dripped from his mouth. He had torn one of his fellow's throats out and was eating him.

Seeing Rosnick and Zanzar, the mad ghoul threw itself at them. Rosnick met the charge head on with the longsword. But the thing pounced on him before he could raise it, tackling him to the deck and raking at his flesh with ragged nails.

The ghastly monstrosity's jaws champed, and saliva flew from its lips, which gibbered within inches of Rosnick's throat. Strong, dark hands seized the thing, pulling it away kicking and screaming, a serpentine tongue lolling from between its blistering lips.

The crew was upon it, hacking with furious bloodlust till it lay broken and mangled in pieces. They severed the head, which continued to bite and make snarling faces for at least a minute before whatever wicked curse kept it alive expired.

"It's that devil weed you both imbibe," said Keeve. "I'm a fool to trust a captain like you—you and your barbarian mate. We leave now."

"Hold your tongue, Keeve," Zanzar hissed. "Can you navigate these forests? We'll be killed fast enough that way."

"I refuse to die in an evil place. To hell with the sails. We march."

"You might remember, Keeve, that part of the agreement is you only get your portion if you fulfill the contract."

"What do contracts or money matter here, now?"

A heavy flapping noise diverted their attention, and the first of the flying apes alighted on a tree limb over the still, moonlit surface of the Nag. Its fierce eyes glowed pale. Two more landed beside it, and then there were more all around the crippled ship. The sky was black with their twisted forms. The triangles of their leathery wings licked the air like black flames. Then, shadowy men emerged from the forest bearing spears. The fast-dwindling crew of the *Hell Cat* formed a circle in the middle of the deck, and in an instant the savages and their vile apes came at them.

Rosnick heard the burbling gasp of the Karkunman beside him as an ape thing took his throat in its jaws. But Rosnick did not allow his attention to be deterred. He fought, cutting and parrying, his sword moving in a continual rhythm that was now so rehearsed it took no thought. He still fought with the same berserker rage even when the entire crew was either wounded or dead. As he turned to defend against someone or something that emerged in his peripheral vision, he felt the numbing sting of the end of a spear shaft slam into the side of his head, and he was unconscious.

The *Hell Cat* listed from side to side like the bulk of a great elephantine skeleton. There was silence, but from the mast hung the head of Zanzar. On the deck of the ship the crew had been cut to pieces. Not a soul survived. Keeve's eyeless face stared back at him, his mouth agape in a final, unholy cry. Rosnick touched his own body to ensure he was corporeal.

The storm ripped and tossed the ship. Rosnick gazed up at the head of Zanzar, the once mighty queen of the Nag. Below the mast where her head hung lay her body, broken and twisted in a puddle of gore. Her cutlass, covered in blood, lay near her, as did the bodies of those she cut down in the fray. The arms and gutted torsos of the Karkunmen crew were strewn about, and the savages squatted about on their haunches, lips smacking as they gorged themselves on dead flesh.

Then, as if in answer to some distant call or need, a group of the naked killers lifted Rosnick onto their shoulders and carried him into the forest.

When the darkness cleared, he was in a marble chamber, incense smoking in golden braziers. Tall curtains, gilded with tassels of the finest silk, covered an archway. A tall man with long, muscular arms and a band of gold around his head reclined on a purple divan across a leopard pelt, holding a goblet of wine.

"Welcome to the land of dead warriors," said the man, hoisting the goblet and drinking.

One of the curtains was pulled aside, and the nubile girl from Rosnick's strange Yanish weed dream stepped forward into the room, trailed by the scent of her jasmine perfume.

"You want to touch her, Uplander? Be my guest," said the man.

Rosnick burned with the desire to feel her soft flesh in his arms. He stood and stepped toward her, and she glided up to him.

"Hold her, Uplander. Hold her, forever. Forever."

The man's voice began to crack and almost peel away, if sounds could be said to do so. The girl's warm body became cold, and her face shriveled and shrank, eyes bulging and staring back at him from dead sockets. Soon, he was holding the desiccated remains of a corpse, and it held him, held him strong. Try as he might, he could not pull away, and her fingers began to elongate and stretch, covering his muscled frame from head to toe in twisting vines that pulled him toward the laughing thing that was once a prince, but was now a mummified thing encrusted in cobwebs and calcification. Under the dried visage of its deeply faded features, its eyes flicked open, revealing sheer black orbs like the craters of a dead star. The cruel marble-like eyes invited Rosnick and sang to him of past glories. The grand and horrible fever dreams of the Yanish weed once more flashed through the Uplander's mind's eye.

"Yes, forever, Uplander. We have become close, you and I. Meet your destiny here with me. Become who you know yourself to be, and give me life."

"Rosnick," came Zanzar's silvery voice.

Craning his head around, he saw her standing there, bathed in bright light. Her skin shined, as if the light was coming from her.

"Do you trust me?" she asked.

She closed her eyes, and a blinding incandescence expanded from her in all directions, filling the room with its holy glow. The mummified thing lifted its arms in front of its face with a reptilian hiss. It screamed, and with a terrible sigh tore itself away from the wall. There was a scuttling and a hissing as the vines released Rosnick and recoiled in pain. He rolled away as they scuttled and searched for him, fiendishly slithering over the ground as if on the trail of some scent.

Zanzar held up a sword. She threw it to him. The handle burned with a glowing fire, yet the weapon did not harm him. Turning his attention to the plant, Rosnick cut through the seeking vines with deft strokes, the wicked boughs falling to the floor and writhing like severed tentacles. The Uplander hewed with the might and speed of a tiger. His forearms were slick with the juices from the cut vines. The stench turned his belly with its familiar tang of the Yanish drug, and he dropped the blade as the vines once again sought purchase on his limbs.

The mummified specter closed its eyes as if savoring the blood of the Uplander. Its mouth opened to reveal a black maw with sharp fangs. Rosnick could see vines writhing beneath the wrappings of its grave vestments. The vines tightened around his arms and legs and pulled him toward the wicked thing. It opened its arms like a lover.

A fierce light beamed from behind, like the corona of an eclipse. Rosnick risked a glance over his shoulder. Bathed within the fierce light was the figure of Zanzar aglow in fire. The lich king hissed, bringing its bandaged arms up to shield its sightless face. The light shot forth into the dark orbs in the deep brow of its slitted head, and it reared back. The plants released Rosnick, and he drove forward with his sword, bringing it down heavy across the dead thing's chest.

The blade cut through it. The thing toppled to the floor in a pile of bandages and dust.

Rosnick materialized out of the bizarre vision, focusing his energy on who he was and his physicality, breaking free of whatever chemical or mystical spell held him. He no longer had the sword, and he was in the pit. The flying ape creatures were assaulting him from all sides. Blood ran down his arms and his torso in rivulets. The vision of Zanzar came to him again, somewhere in the center of his mind, and she was calm, slow and easy, like the summer wind. In a burst of murderous rage, Rosnick fought. One of the apes swooped down at him, and he met its brutish glare with a bass war cry. Gripping the loathsome creature's throat, Rosnick pressed his thumbs into its windpipe and slammed its head into the stone floor repeatedly until its brains spilled out. Two were on his back, tearing at his numbed flesh with their black, needle-like claws.

Rosnick bucked like an Upland bull, flinging the two vile creatures from his back. Once down, Rosnick wasted no time, and with a battle-charged ululation, he leapt on the first one and sank his teeth into its neck, gouging out a rag of flesh and spitting it out. The neck wound gushed, and the creature died quickly. Two more came at him, but he was riding a wave of berserker fury. He smashed both of their heads together, and the floor of the pit was now laden with brain matter and skull fragments.

The monkey things that remained retreated in fear, and in many ways, Rosnick was the most fearful being that day. He looked up at the natives who screamed and chanted bloodlust around the edge of the pit. They leapt about, spears in hand, in some violent war dance. One of them hurled a spear at the Uplander.

Rosnick feinted to the left, dodging the point of the spear, and catching the polearm in his heavy hands with the strength and agility of a jaguar. Rosnick looked up at the raving savage, and with a scream of bloodcurdling rage he hefted the spear, and with every muscle in his body, hurled the missile into the savage's chest and out his back. The tribesman rolled forward into the pit and landed broken and akimbo on the stone floor.

Rosnick pulled the spear out of the native's body, and with the power of a great mountain gorilla, pulled himself up and out of the pit. At the sight of the battle-crazed Uplander covered in blood and viscera, the savages made a path for him.

"I have killed your god!" he shouted. "I have destroyed him, just as you have destroyed my only love and my crew. There are many of you, but so help you if you dare. For I will take as many of you with me into the gates of death as I can. Let me pass."

He passed through them, striding with confidence beyond their ranks toward the edge of the city. But the sudden shock did not last long, and behind him, Rosnick heard them scream, and the crowd chanted, ruffled braids of colorful feathers shaking and winding in their hair. Two of them broke free of the pack, running toward Rosnick with their spears, and soon the rest followed.

The Uplander ran the rest of the way across the small city and into the tree line. He tore through the trees, into the thick heat of the jungle evening, pushing his tired body onward as best he could.

Soon he felt a cold wind on his face, and the forest opened up. He was standing on the edge of a cliff over the Nag. He stopped, gazing down toward the treacherous sea so far below, the waves crashing up against the cliff wall. He could not jump.

But oh yes, he could.

He turned back to see the savages appearing out of the forest, longbows at the ready. Their gray figures flew toward him on hardened feet, ululating their untamed cry. As soon as the lead pair drew back the gut, the arrow nocked and aimed, Rosnick leapt over the edge and fell, the wooden shafts of arrows hurtling past him into the night winds.

There was darkness, and once more, he dreamed. In it, Zanzar held him in her arms. There was the soft warmth of her hand on his back, and she whispered in his ear, but he couldn't understand, at least not in words.

She released him and stood before him bathed in light, just before stepping onto a golden longboat with dragon prows, as he felt himself floating downward, and his vision faded.

Rosnick lifted his head from the waves and gasped air. His senses were alive. He felt the cold sting of the waves, and the sublime crack of thunder cut through the night. The Uplander paddled, fought to stay above the waves. Something white appeared in the distance. As it drew closer, he saw sails bobbing out of the sea like the wings of Valkyries, and Rosnick forced his eyes to stay open, to resist the death watch of the gods. A hand reached out, and he grabbed the strong wrist, and he was pulled up onto the deck of the *Alizarin Witch*.

-End-

Meet the Author
Tim Gerstmar

Thanks for taking the time to answer a few questions. Start by giving our readers a short bio. Who are you and how long have you been writing?

I'm a high school English and art teacher, and I work at an international school in Taiwan. I have been writing and creating visual art all my life. But I've been more focused on the writing for the past twenty years or so.

Congratulations on placing a story in the pages of Savage Realms. We get inundated with stories every month and only a few are chosen. Is this your first story with Savage Realms? Have you published other stories in previous magazines? If so tell the readers which issue they can find those stories in.

This is not my first story published in Savage Realms. My story 'The Glass Crypt', featuring the same character, is in the January 2022 issue. I have written a number of flash fiction pieces for Shotgun Honey and other online magazines. I also have a creepy little horror story in the fall

2012 issue of Dark Gothic Resurrected Magazine, which is available on amazon. You can also find my novels The Gunfighters and Unitan 29: Memories of a spaceman on amazon.

Tell us a little more about your main character? What motivates them? And what motivates you to write about them?

Rosnick is a Conan-style mercenary, motivated primarily by money and hedonistic impulses. In 'The Glass Crypt', he was an older guy who wasn't doing all that well with money because of his frivolous spending habits, so he is forced to take on an opportunity that could, and does, prove rather deadly. I liked the character, and I wanted to show him during his younger years, which I did in this story.

Will we be seeing any more of this character in the future?

It is possible. I do have a few sketches featuring Rosnick that I tinker with now and then. Off and on I've played with the idea of compiling and publishing a collection of tales about him. Similarly with Conan, the stories would range throughout his life and career.

Being published is a rare thing. Some writers work their whole life and never make it happen. You did. Give other aspiring writers a little advice and hope for the future.

I don't know if I feel qualified to give this kind of advice, because I think it varies. That said, I had an excellent professor in art school who would preface all his assignments by saying to make sure whatever you do you enjoy, because if you don't enjoy it, nobody else will. I think that is good artistic advice in general, because if you like what you did you have already won. So, only write something you enjoy and wish to see in print, and write it to the absolute best of your current abilities. Then send it out to places you think might be interested in the kind of work you do. The rest is out of your hands, but you have to try, and you must have fun.

Finally, what are you reading right now? Is it any good? And what's the one sword and sorcery story every fan should read at least once before they die?

I'm reading The Tropic of Cancer, *by Henry Miller, and I am enjoying it. The sword and sorcery story I would recommend is* 'Queen of the Black Coast', *by Robert E. Howard. I have to recommend that one, because my story is an homage to it.*

Discover the Savage Realms Game Books

Enter the prolific worlds of...
SAVAGE REALMS
Gamebooks
Available on
Amazon and
DriveThruRPG
savagerealmsgamebooks.com

CURSED

BY CARL WALMSLEY

"You're sure about this?" Gallarin stared mistrustfully down the narrow track that led through the rocks and into the prison.

"We need a mage," said Inquisitor Draub, scratching irritably at the sores on his tonsured scalp. "The only ones left alive are here. Follow me."

Although the king had granted Gallarin's request to command the expedition, he was not sure the inquisitor saw it that way.

"Have the men wait here," Gallarin told his second, Caius, and urged his horse after the inquisitor.

Sheer slopes enveloped the twisting track. Two rows of *vigilant sisters* stood atop these, their faces daubed with script from the *Book of*

- *Benediction*. Gallarin had heard their singing almost a mile off, while leading his troops through the wasteland which housed the prison. He had thought it beautiful, but now, as it resonated around him, he noticed a discordant quality that made his teeth ache.

"They do not speak," said the inquisitor, "but save their voices only for song."

Gallarin considered himself a pious enough man, but had never understood the more extreme tenets of the Faith. "Why?"

The inquisitor sneered as if Gallarin were a schoolboy who had not finished his homework. "The song helps to control the prisoners, Captain."

"I thought the null-iron did that." Gallarin had already noticed that the rock walls glinted with deposits of the rare ore, native to this region. Within the prison itself, every wall would be laced with the metal.

"It does," allowed the inquisitor, "but one cannot be too careful when dealing with *abominations*. Remember, if even one of these prisoners escaped, the entire realm would be in jeopardy."

They passed beyond a heavy metal door, thrown open for their approach. Gallarin wondered if it was crafted from null-iron. He carried a shield forged from the metal—a badge of his office—and knew that it was worth more than his father's estate.

Past the door was a stone gatehouse, constructed with murder holes and arrow slits that would not be out of place in a border fortress. A figure peered down at them from a high, well-screened balcony.

"I am Inquisitor Draub."

Gallarin supressed a flash of irritation at not announcing himself first.

The guard bobbed obsequiously. "Yes, your grace. The warden is expecting you. He has assembled the prisoners in the yard."

Half a dozen figures stood in the centre of the dusty courtyard, their feet and wrists chained to metal loops in the ground. One man had iron tubes covering his hands; another woman had been blindfolded; a third had apparently been forced to his knees, blood flowing from a freshly cracked lip.

Three dozen guards encircled the group. Half carried bows, with arrows nocked. The others wore mail and had their weapons drawn.

"These are the only ones who would agree to hear your proposal, Inquisitor," intoned the warden, a tall, slender man with a long, neatly plaited beard. He spoke with a soft, almost embarrassed tone. "And I fear this one," he gestured at the man on his knees, "may not have been entirely sincere."

Draub stepped past the line of guards, several of whom shifted their feet nervously.

Gallarin knew that dealing with mages was the inquisitor's trade, so it made sense to let him take the lead in this.

"Do you wish to earn your freedom?" Draub asked the prisoners.

The man with a bloodied lip hawked and spat. A red gobbet landed close to the inquisitor's black boot. "There's no place for mages in your world."

"That is true," said Draub. "But if you agree to help me, your sentence will be commuted to banishment. You will be free to leave Bretayne and make a new life."

The prisoners exchanged glances.

"Bollocks! Who'd trust a bloody inquisitor?" said the bleeding man.

Draub snatched a bow from the nearest guard, drew the string to his cheek, and put an arrow through the man's chest. The prisoner coughed, looked as if he would say something, and sagged back onto his haunches.

"This is all that awaits you here," shouted Draub. "Fast or slow, you will die within these walls. Or—you can come with me. Which is it to be?"

The prisoners looked at the corpse and then amongst themselves. A pale-skinned man with black lips finally stepped forward, followed by a slender woman, her shaven head decorated with strange sigils.

Draub handed the bow to the warden. "Throw the others back in their cells."

"That one," said the warden, gesturing to the black-lipped man, "is particularly dangerous, your grace."

"I hope so," said Draub.

"How much are we going to tell them about the curse?" asked Gallarin, watching the two mages being loaded into a wagon.

"For now, nothing," said Draub.

"I disagree." Gallarin was already tired of the inquisitor trying to make every decision. He was here as an advisor, nothing more. "If the mages are to help us, they need time to figure out who's responsible for the curse. We can't await the moment when they are to be of use and then spring it on them." Gallarin was pleased to find that his reasoning made sense.

Draub sighed. "Shield Captain Gallarin…"

A shout from one of the soldiers halted their discussion. The black-lipped mage had tossed his manacles from the back of the wagon, sparking something of a panic amongst the troops guarding him. They were only a few dozen yards from the track that led into the prison, but the mage's power was clearly returning.

Gallarin paced towards the wagon as the unbound mage placed his hands over his ears and glared up at the *benevolent sisters*, still singing from atop the walls. The female mage, in stark contrast, was reclining in the back of the wagon, her head resting on her chained hands.

Gallarin tossed the broken chains into the cart and hopped up beside the pale mage. "Allow me to introduce myself. I am Shield Captain Mathrick Gallarin. I command these troops and have been tasked with escorting you to the western border where—if you help me—I will release you. If you try to escape, however, or refuse to co-operate, it is my job to take you back to your cell."

The mage took his hands from his ears and Gallarin saw that his lips, fingernails and even his tongue were the dark purple of a livid bruise.

"I thank you for the gift of your name," said the mage, his voice surprisingly soft. "I am Mor'kar'kuul. Tell me what you want, Mathrick Gallarin, and I will tell you if I can provide it."

Inquisitor Draub approached the cart, carrying a polished wooden box that he had taken from the baggage train. When Mor'kar'kuul saw it, his dark eyes widened.

"You were led to believe that this had been destroyed, mage." Draub opened one of several drawers in the box, revealing an intricately carved mask.

Mor'kar'kuul stood and extended a hand, but Draub snapped the drawer shut. "If you disobey even one of my orders, this will burn."

The mage sat slowly.

"I have something of yours, as well," Draub said to the second mage.

If she heard, she did nothing to reveal the fact.

Inquisitor Draub handed the box to a servant and made a show of taking a small metallic sphere from a pouch on his belt. He placed it inside one of the drawers so that a fuse poked out. He mimed an explosion with his hands. "Are we clear, mage?"

Mor'kar'kuul glared at the inquisitor for several seconds, then nodded.

Draub was already walking away. "Get your men moving, Captain."

There were three hundred troops in the column that marched westwards from the parched lands. As they advanced, tufts of hardy grass appeared between the rocks, then stunted bushes and, finally, small trees hunched over like beggars. It was late summer, but there was no vibrancy in any of the plants, and the column was a full ten miles from the prison before Gallarin saw a bird.

"It's the mages," said Draub, who had chosen to ride with the captain at the front of the line. "Despite our best efforts, their taint bleeds into the land. That's why no crops will grow in this part of Bretayne."

Gallarin had heard as much before.

"What's in the box?" Gallarin asked. He had not known about the items the inquisitor had shown the mages.

"A collection of masks. Each bestows some unnatural power upon the wearer."

"And you intend to give it to him?"

"If it enables us to end the curse." Draub clutched the symbol at his neck. "Princess Zamina will give birth in less than a month. The future heir must be...*whole*."

Gallarin understood the significance of a healthy royal child—Zamina's babe would secure the succession and another generation of peace—but his thoughts were of his own wife. Jollista had experienced none of the pain that troubled many pregnant women across Bretayne. That did not mean she would be spared. As far as Gallarin knew, there had been no *natural* births in months. Many of the mothers had not survived labour...

Gallarin forced these thoughts aside. He would not serve the realm, nor Jollista and their unborn child, by fretting. He needed to carry out his orders. Once they reached the western border, they could identify the source of the curse and end it.

2

The western province was famed for its beauty, and two day's ride from the prison, Gallarin led the column past lush fields and orchards. Smallfolk waved at them from the fields as they gathered the harvest. A few even lined the road to watch them pass. It was very different from the parched lands further east that had been blighted by magic.

"Send out troops to top up our supplies," Gallarin instructed Caius. They were well-stocked, but three hundred men and horses could eat a lot and would be venturing beyond the border.

Soon after, Caius returned looking concerned. "Sir, the villagers say that the harvest has been less abundant this year." Caius gestured towards a small line of locals bearing baskets of fruit. "They can spare a little, but claim any more will leave them short for the winter."

Gallarin shrugged. "Collect a tithe from each village we pass through. Nothing that will leave the people starving."

Gallarin wondered if the diminished yield was linked to the taint that Draub had mentioned. Bretayne had imprisoned its mages years ago, and the land certainly looked fertile, so he could not see how. It was possible that this was another symptom of the curse. Reluctantly, Gallarin accepted that this was something he should discuss with Draub and rode back along the line to find him.

Near the centre of the column was the wagon transporting the two mages. The woman was gazing at the fields, her face placid, while Mor'kar'kuul watched the captain approach. The previous night, Gallarin had assigned thirty men to guard the mages while the rest of the expedition slept. So far, neither had done anything to cause him concern. The offer of banishment in exchange for help ending the curse was a good one, and he hoped that they saw the sense in this.

The afternoon calm was broken by a sudden shriek. Summoning a handful of men, Gallarin galloped towards the sound. It was a woman's voice, plaintive and shrill. Dismounting outside a simple wooden shack, Gallarin slammed open the door.

Within, a young woman lay sprawled on her back, grunting and sweating. She was attended by three older women, holding cloths and a pail of water, but overseeing the birth was Inquisitor Draub.

"If you intend to stay, Captain, please close the door."

Gallarin hesitated for an instant, waved his men away, and stepped inside. One of the women bustled past and, moving aside, Gallarin clattered against a shelf, knocking over a pot. "Perhaps, I should…"

The woman screamed again, the sound stretching out into a whine that left the captain wincing. A baby mewled, and Draub whisked something from between the woman's legs and bundled it inside a cloth. One of the women in the room gasped. Another turned away, her eyes wide.

The mother, exhausted and sweat-sodden, reached for the child. "Give him to me…"

Draub stood and, without looking at her, marched from the room. As the new mother began to wail, Gallarin hurried after the inquisitor.

"Inquisitor Draub!"

Draub turned, a dozen paces from the shack, the newborn in his arms hidden entirely beneath the tightly bound cloth. "I will deal with this, Captain. See to it that none of the women try to follow."

Gallarin watched him go, unsure what to do until it was too late to do anything. Along the way, Draub snatched a spade from the soil.

Outside the shack, Gallarin raised a hand to the door. He heard sobbing inside and for one dreadful moment the voice sounded like

Jollista's. He closed his eyes and forced the thought away. Turning sharply, he left the women to their pain.

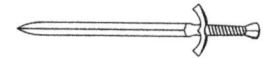

For the rest of the day, the expedition travelled west through more settlements where locals gathered their crops. Again, though, Caius brought reports of lower yields. And they passed an orchard where the apples were rotting on the branch.

Draub had resumed his position at the head of the column, but Gallarin had no wish to see the man. If he did, he would feel compelled to ask about the baby. Instead, he fell back towards the centre.

"What happened?" The question came from the female mage and startled Gallarin for, though he heard her voice clearly, she was several carts back. The captain slowed his horse, until she pulled alongside.

"A woman was with child?" she asked.

Gallarin nodded.

"Was it a difficult birth?"

"It was. It did not end well."

Gallarin saw the concern on the woman's face which, despite her lack of hair, was shapely and kind.

"I would have helped."

"You will have a chance to help, soon enough."

"And how will that be, Mathrick Gallarin?" Mor'kar'kuul had been listening to the conversation and now shifted to the closer side of the wagon.

Gallarin glanced along the column towards the inquisitor and, with a flash of annoyance, reminded himself that he did not need permission to speak with the prisoners.

"There is a curse. Babies born in Bretayne are *unnatural*."

"They do not survive?" asked the woman.

"They do not."

Both mages regarded Gallarin intently. Side by side, the contrast between them was stark. Mor'kar'kuul had pale, bloodless flesh, exacerbated by the colour of his lips and hair. The woman had coppery skin and no hair at all; not even eyebrows. The tattoos on her scalp were as bright and colourful as a fresh canvas.

"The western borders have been attacked," Gallarin continued. "The lands beyond are lawless and wild. There are...*people* there who could create this curse."

The choice of words did not disguise what they were discussing. Only a mage could conjure a curse.

"So, you want us to kill our own?" Mor'kar'kuul said, sitting bolt upright.

"I have no desire to kill anyone," Gallarin said, earnestly. "Before this posting, I was *first shield* to the royal household. My job is to keep people alive. But children are dying from this curse."

My child may die.

They rode on in silence, and Gallarin gave them time to consider his words.

"If we help end this curse, you will free us?" asked the woman.

"You have my word..." Gallarin realised that he did not know the woman's name and asked her.

"I am Thestia." She entwined her fingers, touching them to her heart and then her head.

It was an old-fashioned gesture of friendship. Gallarin remembered his grandfather doing it whenever he met a friend or neighbour.

"I have no wish to see newborns die," Thestia said. "If I can help end this curse, I will. But I must warn you. We will not be welcome in the lands to the west."

Gallarin's troops were well-drilled and, when he gave the order to stop for the night, three dozen broad blue tents arose swiftly in neat lines, while cooking fires were prepared. As before, a contingent of watchful soldiers stood guard over the two mages.

"How did they respond?" asked Draub, taking a seat beside Gallarin's campfire.

The captain had hoped to eat his meal with Caius and discuss his plans for the next day. He also disliked the notion that Draub had been watching him.

Caius rose, dipped his head to each man, and headed towards the nearest fire.

"The woman, Thestia, has promised to help. She showed concern for the pregnant woman and her child."

"So, you trust her?" asked Draub.

Gallarin shrugged, feeling again the urge to oppose the inquisitor's view. "Neither one has tried to escape."

"Of course not." Draub took a bowl and dipped it into the steaming stew. It covered his fingers as much as the bowl, but he showed no sign of discomfort. "They will not try to escape until we reach the border. What's the use of being free inside Bretayne, with three hundred soldiers at hand?"

Gallarin considered arguing that mages might well have a way to slip away, but knew it would sound churlish.

"I understand that you requested this posting," said Draub, half-emptying his bowl in a few scoops.

Gallarin wondered whether the inquisitor knew about his wife. If not, he saw no point in telling him. "As *first shield* it is my duty protect Princess Zamina, and her unborn child."

Draub continued to eat. "Based on what I saw this afternoon, the child may already be spoiled."

The inquisitor's words caused Gallarin to spill some of the stew onto his hand. Unlike Draub, he winced at the pain.

The inquisitor smiled, and Gallarin thought he had never seen a less convincing expression. "Still, let us be optimistic."

"Indeed. We must have faith," said Gallarin.

This time, the mirth on Draub's features was sincere. "Good night, Captain."

3

Gallarin rubbed his eyes, wearily. It was five days since they had left the prison, and he had not slept well once. However far they travelled each day, it would not be enough. Jollista had been seven months pregnant when he last saw her. There was still time to find the source of the curse and end it but he knew babies could arrive early, and the expedition had set out almost two weeks ago…

Gallarin's eye was drawn to a pale stone marker beside the road: *498 miles to Dun Caereg*—the capital of Bretayne. If that was right, they should already have reached the border. Kicking his horse into a canter, Gallarin moved ahead of the column, and within a mile encountered another strange sight.

To either side of the road, new buildings were under construction. The edge of a nearby wood had been hacked back, leaving hundreds of pale stumps. Teams of men were assembling a dry wall around the perimeter of a new settlement. The frame of a mill lay stretched out on the grass beside a swift waterway. In all, there were more than a hundred craftsmen and labourers, along with dozens of children performing menial tasks.

The captain watched them toil while he waited for the column to catch up. Draub led them, his ash-coloured armour making him stand out from the soldier's pale blue tabards.

"Impressive, isn't it, Captain?"

Gallarin waited until he was close enough to speak softly. "I studied the maps of Bretayne before we set out. The border…"

"Is a transient thing. What is wilderness, but land crying out for the touch of civilisation?" The inquisitor swept his hand over the landscape. "In another year, there will be crops here, livestock. A flourishing community."

"Who is responsible for this?" Gallarin asked.

"The work was commissioned by the Crown, with the support of the Faith." Draub pointed at an outline of stone blocks on a patch of high ground. "A new temple will rise here. These people will be nourished, body and soul."

"But why move these people here?"

"You know why, Captain." It was Draub's turn to speak softly.

"The failing crops?"

The inquisitor nodded. "There is no organised government here. The people who wander these lands are vagrants. They build nothing. Villages like this will have a civilising effect of them, I have no doubt. Many will even find their way to the Faith."

The column had now passed the settlement, and Gallarin peered into the distance. "And those who do not?"

"Will retreat further into the wilderness," said Draub. "For now, at least."

It was another twenty miles, past two more fledgling villages, before the inquisitor announced that they had reached the border. One of his servants set a marker stone beside the road. *519 miles to Dun Caereg.*

"Your men must be wary tonight, Captain. We have reached the edge of the world." Draub glared at the stretches of ancient forest, thick with shadow as night approached. "Pay particular attention to the mages. We did not come all this way for nothing."

Despite his soldiers' need for sleep, Gallarin increased the watch to forty men. He did not think that the mages would try to escape, but flinched at the thought of telling Draub they had. *Did I not warn you, Captain?*

Regardless of what Gallarin tried, sleep would not come. His mind was a hornet's nest: every thought and concern stung him into wakefulness. *"The child may already be spoiled,"* Draub had said. That thought chilled Gallarin. Then there was the movement of the border. Why had he not been told about that? Rising from his bedroll, Gallarin drained a flask of water, and, as if the liquid had passed straight through him, he felt the need to empty his bladder.

As soon as the night air touched his skin, Gallarin felt calmer. The smells and sounds of the men and horses were a familiar comfort. He had spent five years at the royal palace. But, before that, he had campaigned, fending off attacks from the northern kingdoms. That had been a simpler time. At least he had known who he was fighting.

Moving a few yards from his tent, Gallarin spotted one of the sentries. He whistled to alert the man to his approach. When the guard did not turn, Gallarin offered him a soft greeting. Still, he did not move.

Touching the sentry's shoulder, Gallarin saw that two spears had been driven through his chest, propping him upright like a scarecrow. Blood seeped from his slack jaw.

Gallarin reached for his sword, realised he had left it in his tent, and cursed softly. He ducked down into the tall grass. Doing so, he came face to face with a figure lying hidden in the brush. The shape blew something from its palm and Gallarin felt his eyes and throat ignite. The captain threw himself back. He could not to breathe, let alone call out. Wheeling away, Gallarin banged his hands together, trying to attract attention. Something smashed into him, and he thudded sideways. Hands fumbled and tried to pin him down. Blindly, Gallarin lashed out, feeling his knee connect. He repeated the motion twice more and someone squawked in pain. Other sounds echoed around him, followed by shouts of warning, and Gallarin heard the ringing of the alarm bell.

Lurching upright, the captain swung his fists blindly and bounded away. He needed to put some distance between himself and his attacker. He rubbed his eyes frantically; the pain was horrible, and Gallarin experienced a sudden terror that the blindness might be permanent. A blur of shapes appeared, though: blue tents, hazy figures rushing through the night. Gallarin was still fighting for breath and his throat was coppery with blood.

Stumbling towards the closest tent, Gallarin threw himself down and scrambled under the canvas. There were half a dozen men inside, clambering from their blankets and seizing weapons. Startled by the captain's sudden appearance, one of them raised a weapon. Gallarin tried to calm him, but his voice was a croak. The man's sword arced over Gallarin's head as he hurled himself forward.

"Wait!" One of the other soldier's seized the swordsman's arm and pointed at Gallarin, whose face was now visible in the lantern-light.

"I'm sorry, Captain..." the swordsman stammered.

Gallarin waved the apology away and motioned for the men to get outside, touching his throat to show that he could not speak. As they moved, one of the soldiers handed Gallarin a sword.

Outside, several tents were aflame. Against the blaze, dark figures moved and fought and Gallarin saw that this was a sizeable assault. He pointed his men towards the nearest melee and led them forward.

In the near-dark, it was difficult to make out who was attacking them. They carried spears and axes and relied on ferocity and speed rather than the discipline of trained ranks. Where they could, Gallarin's men formed shield walls, using the tents to protect their flanks.

"Where are the wizards, captain?"

A rough hand gripped Gallarin's shoulder and he found himself facing the inquisitor. The priest held a morningstar, the metal spikes dark with blood.

Gallarin croaked, something that was almost a word, then turned in the direction of the cart where the mages had been secured. Again, Draub spun him about.

"No! They aren't there!"

Gallarin growled in frustration. His mouth felt like it was full of scalding sand. He shrugged the priest off.

"Sear-rch!" He ripped the word from his throat and, ignoring the priest's words, dashed towards the wagon. Shapes moved around him, distorted shadows in the whirling flames. Some seemed huge and monstrous.

Gallarin found the cart empty, and hurried between the avenues of tents, trying to shut out the sounds of battle and his rising panic. If the mages had escaped, this entire journey would have been for nothing. What then of his daughter and Princess Zamina's child?

Gallarin found Thestia hunched over the body of a wounded man. Her hands were on his chest and, as she spoke, the sigils on her skin shimmered.

Mor'kar'kuul stood a dozen paces away, facing a group of wild-looking figures and a man in a high, antlered helm. Gallarin marvelled at his size. Even without the horns, he stood over seven feet tall.

With a bellow, one of the figures rushed forward. Mor'kar'kuul brought his fingers to his mouth and then flicked something from his hand. The onrushing man slowed, limbs juddering to a halt. He tottered and then slumped to one side, as immobile as a statue.

Gallarin advanced and stood beside the mage, unsure whether he was helping him or apprehending him. Either way, it suddenly did not matter. Horns rang out, loud and clear and, with a suddenness that impressed Gallarin, the attackers withdrew. Volleys of spears deterred any pursuit, and in moments they were vanishing into the darkness.

Instinctively, Gallarin tried to issue an order to secure the perimeter, and winced at the pain in his throat. The mage peered at him quizzically.

"It seems we are both hurt, Mathrick Gallarin." The mage held up a hand, and Gallarin saw that many of his fingernails were missing.

"There is always a price for magic." There was blood on Mor'kar'kuul's lips, and the captain guessed that he had torn them out with his teeth.

Gallarin pointed towards the wagon. He was furious with himself for allowing this ambush; even more so that the mages were free.

"I need my masks, Captain," said Mor'kar'kull. "I will not be able to help you without them."

Gallarin repeated the gesture.

Mor'kar'kuul did not move until Thestia looped an arm through his and gently urged him. "We will return to the wagon, captain."

Gallarin watched them stride away, and saw the wounded man whom Thestia had helped sit up and reach through the tear in his armour to the healed flesh beneath.

4

The attack left thirty-four men dead and almost as many too badly injured to fight. At sun-up, a search of the surrounding area did not reveal a single enemy body. Whoever had attacked them had taken their dead with them. Only the attackers who died inside the camp itself remained. They were men, dressed in furs and leather, skin daubed with mud to help them hide.

Gallarin was listening to the scouts' reports when Draub stomped through the mud towards him. The inquisitor's dark-socketed eyes suggested that, like Gallarin himself, Draub had not slept since the attack.

"What are you doing, Captain?"

Gallarin made a point of completing his orders to Caius before turning to the inquisitor. "I have thirty men that cannot go on. I'm sending them back to the last village. They can take the fallen with them for burial."

"We need every man that can carry a blade. Those that are hurt must struggle on. You've seen what these savages are capable of."

Gallarin considered asking the inquisitor to continue their conversation in private, but there was something in the man's manic expression which dissuaded him. He wanted his troops to hear this exchange.

"I won't throw my men's lives away. A dozen of them won't last the day if they march onwards."

Draub twisted his neck to squint into a tent where injured men were being tended. The motion reminded Gallarin of a vulture surveying its next meal. "Your men will do as they're commanded."

"They will," agreed Gallarin. "And, right now, they have been commanded to make stretchers."

Draub inhaled angrily but, before he could unleash whatever tirade he was preparing, Gallarin continued.

"Whoever attacked us last night is protecting their border. A border that seems to have moved. What response can we expect when we march three companies of armed men into their territory? This is a military operation, under *my* command, and I intend to do what I think best to ensure its success."

The inquisitor's chest rose and fell like a forge bellows, and it was several seconds before he mastered himself. "What are you suggesting, Captain?"

"A small contingent will follow the tracks left by the attackers: myself, ten of my best troops...and the mages. Caius will remain in command of the main force. If we do not return within two days, he will continue the advance. You are free to come with us or to remain here, as you choose."

The inquisitor's gaze was like a lash, and Gallarin felt a sudden kinship with those left alone with Draub in the *Hall of Questions*.

"What makes you think these savages will not simply kill you, Captain?"

"Firstly, they withdrew when the horns sounded. They may not fight like us, but they understand orders. Someone commands them—someone we can talk to."

Draub raised no argument.

"Secondly, they gathered their dead and wounded. That means they are a unified force, quite possibly protecting their homes. Both suggest that these are people we can talk to."

"And what of the curse?" Draub drew the last word into a hiss. "Was it not magic which silenced you earlier?"

Gallarin had drained an entire waterskin, and his throat still burned, but he ignored the pain. "We don't know if they're responsible for the curse. Questioning them might reveal a lot more than killing them."

"Very well," said Draub, finally. "I shall come with you. I have some experience asking questions."

The ancient forest cloaked the land as far east as Gallarin could see. Despite the morning sunlight which settled on its unbroken canopy, the trees beneath looked black.

Raising a hand, Gallarin halted the small contingent of troops. "We make no attempt to remain hidden. No one must think that we try to enter these lands unnoticed."

The five scouts, used to avoiding danger by stealth, looked uncomfortable, while the five spearmen kept their shields high as if marching into battle. Gallarin knew that many of them would be thinking of revenge for the previous night's attack.

"We are here to talk with these people, not fight them."

"An interesting plan, Mathrick Gallarin," murmured Mor'kar'kuul, motioning towards the forest with scabbed fingertips. "I wonder if you will be given a chance to explain it."

Gallarin had brought his horse to the edge of the forest, and now unbuckled one of its paniers. "Do you give me your word that you will help me end this curse in exchange for your freedom?" He aimed the question at both of the mages.

"I do," said Thestia.

Mor'kar'kuul nodded.

Uncinching the null-iron shield presented to him on the day he was named *first shield*, Gallarin handed it to Draub. It was the price for the inquisitor's cooperation in his plan.

Draub fastened the shield onto his left arm and glared at the mages, as if daring them to use their magic against him now.

From inside the first saddlebag, Gallarin retrieved a wooden box and offered it to Mor'kar'kuul. The mage took it without hesitation. From the second panier, the captain took a large pouch, tied at the top with a leather thong, and presented it to Thestia. She unbound the bag and reached inside. Sand trickled through her fingers and Gallarin noticed how it sparkled in the sunlight.

Thestia repeated the gesture of friendship she had made before. "The magic here is strong. If you wish, I can use it to conceal us."

Gallarin shook his head. Flexing the fingers of his left hand, which felt suddenly empty, he followed the tracks towards the treeline.

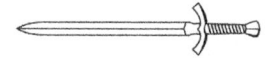

Fifty paces into the forest, Gallarin realised that his group could not have travelled quietly even if they had wished to. The spearmen and Draub blundered through the undergrowth, using their broad shields to force a path. Even the scouts, chosen for their nimbleness, found their dark breeches snagging on thorns and low branches. Only Thestia seemed able to move unhindered through the dense woodland, selecting a path between obstructions. Mor'kar'kuul had the sense to follow her; and Gallarin chose to follow him.

All around were plants that Gallarin did not recognise, despite his years of travel. Pale, crescent-shaped fungi and blood-red flowers sprouted from clefts in the bark. Where the branches stirred, feathery seed pods drifted down to catch on clothing and redden skin. Gallarin brushed against a tree and an insect as big as his hand unfolded barbed legs, grating them together like the hiss of a whetstone.

Mor'kar'kuul chuckled, softly. "He does not welcome you, Mathrick Gallarin."

They pressed onwards, moving sideways as much as forwards until, with rising frustration, Gallarin realised that he was no longer certain which way led back to the treeline.

"Wait." Gallarin had traversed woods before, but nothing like this.

"Second thoughts, Captain?" There was a crunch as Draub used the null-iron shield to bludgeon aside a thicket and stomp closer.

Gallarin could not lead his troops further into this forest. Draub watched him expectantly.

Gallarin raised his voice as high as his wounded throat would allow. "I wish to talk."

His words felt muffled by the branches and he called again, over and over, until a crash of movement drew every eye.

A hulking shape forced a path through the brush. There was a crack as a sapling sagged and then snapped under the weight of a bear's forepaws. The animal clattered forward, rose up on its hind legs, and roared a challenge. The sound was met by an equally ferocious bellow, and Gallarin saw that Mor'kar'kuul had stepped forward to meet the bear. The mage's face was hidden beneath one of his masks. Gallarin gawped as the mage's jaw distended and stretched to impossible proportions, a long leonine tongue emerging like a snake.

The bear closed its mouth, dropped to all fours, and stared wide-eyed at Mor'kar'kuul. Lowering its head, it slunk away into the trees, its massive hindquarters swaying ponderously.

Mor'kar'kuul peeled back the mask as he turned to the group, revealing a glimpse of some hideous visage before he was a man once more. "If you intend to do something like that again, Mathrick Gallarin, I would appreciate a warning."

Before Gallarin could answer, another voice carried clearly through the forest. "If you truly wish to talk, walk towards the light."

A golden gleam shone instantly through the westward trees.

"Keep your weapons low," Gallarin told his men, doing his best to act as if this was precisely what he had expected, and set off at once.

The forest seemed suddenly less tangled, and Gallarin soon emerged into a clearing of lush grass, vivid in the morning sunshine. At its centre sat a slender man, arrayed in a deer-pelt cloak. A golden circlet rested on his brow, flashing in the morning light. Behind the man stood the tall, antler-helmed figure that had led the attack on the camp. He was flanked by warriors in furs and hides, carrying axes and spears. They seemed small next to the antlered man but several were as tall as the captain.

There was a crunch as Draub kicked his way into the clearing, followed by the spearmen. The scouts, fanning out, emerged more quietly, while Mor'kar'kuul and Hestia stood to either side of the captain.

"Sit," said the figure on the grass.

Seeing that the man was unarmed, Gallarin unbuckled his sword belt, placed it on the ground and sat opposite him. "I am Mathrick Gallarin."

The seated man nodded almost imperceptibly, then took a moment to regard each of those that Gallarin had brought with him. His eyes lingered on Thestia.

The mage returned the gaze, bowed low, then spoke in a language that Gallarin did not understand. The seated man smiled and nodded.

"You said that you wished to talk," said Thestia. "Our host is waiting for you to do so."

Gallarin smiled an awkward thanks and cleared his throat.

"I am from Bretayne, a servant of his majesty, King Agathenes..." Gallarin hesitated as the antlered figure growled, shifting his weight from one enormous leg to another. "There is a curse affecting the people of my kingdom. Babies are being born deformed. Most do not survive for more than a few hours. Those that do are unnatural. It has been this way for months. None of our scholars or physicians can explain it. I am here...looking for answers."

Gallarin knew this was, at best, a version of the truth. He had been dispatched to find those responsible for the curse and kill them. Somewhere along the way, he had become convinced that this was not the answer.

"Why come here?" asked the seated man.

"The curse is magical in nature. Since we have no mages in Bretayne, the curse must come from elsewhere. Recently, there has been conflict between our people..." Gallarin knew that he was coming dangerously close to making an accusation. "For my part," said Gallarin, "I regret that conflict. I wish to talk so that we might resolve any dispute peacefully."

The antlered man hawked and spat and those alongside him shifted restlessly. In response, Gallarin's own spearmen lifted their shields, as did Inquisitor Draub.

The seated man turned his head from one group to another and then spoke to Thestia in the unknown language. Back and forth they went, and Gallarin felt a sheen of sweat prickle his shoulders.

"What is she saying?" hissed Draub.

Gallarin did not answer. He did not know.

"He knows the cause of the curse," said Thestia, finally. "But he will not tell you. He says that you will not believe him."

"What? But that's why I'm here..." Gallarin stared at the seated man, who met his gaze with unsettling calm.

Ahead and behind, the two groups of warriors continued to regard each other warily.

"King Agathenes' daughter is pregnant," said Gallarin.

The seated man did not react.

Gallarin recalled the newborn, taken by Draub before its life could begin. He thought of the mother's scream, the way it reminded him of Jollista. "My own wife is pregnant. I am here because I want the truth. Whatever truth will save our unborn child."

The seated man's eyes were green. Green like the grass in the sunshine. Green like the forest. Green like the distant sea...

Gallarin blinked, feeling as if he came back to himself from far away. The seated man seemed to be looking at him a little differently.

"The people of Bretayne *are* cursed," he said. "And its source is, indeed, magical. But not in the way you think."

"Enough!"

Gallarin was startled to find that Draub had closed to within a few yards, drawing the spearmen with him. "If he will not answer our questions, there are ways to persuade him."

Gallarin sprang up and shoved the inquisitor backwards. Spiteful eyes glared at him over the rim of the null-iron shield. *His* shield.

"Let him finish, Draub."

Gallarin sat, forcing himself to ignore the inquisitor's proximity. "Please, tell me the truth."

"Your land is poisoned," said the seated man. "The energy which nurtures it...replenishes it...has been removed. Now, the land is dying."

Gallarin tried to understand what he was being told. Magic contaminated the world. It blighted crops...everyone knew that. "Are you saying the land *needs* magic?"

"That's a lie," snarled Draub. "Magic is an abomination. Men stealing the power of the Gods!"

The seated man looked at Draub, quizzically. "What strange things you believe."

Draub leapt forward and, distracted, Gallarin reached too late for the inquisitor's arm. There was a dreadful crack as Draub's spiked ball struck the side of the seated man's head. The golden band on his brow was driven deep into his skull and he flopped onto the grass.

"Kill them all," roared the inquisitor.

Gallarin called for them to stop but warriors on either side came together in a clash of weapons. An axe whirled through the air, striking Gallarin's breastplate. He gasped, staggered sideways, but managed to stay on his feet.

"Stop! Stop!"

Gallarin's words were drowned out by the clamour of battle, then the two sides were wrenched apart in a wash of purple light. Mor'kar'kuul stood between them, his face hidden by a silver mask with six violet eyes and long, curved horns.

Only Draub remained standing. The purple light bloomed and then dissipated around his null-iron shield. Grinning coldly, he advanced on the mage.

The mouth of Mor'kar'kuul's mask widened, emitting a gush of purple vapour. A tendril touched one of the spearmen as he clambered to his feet and sent him tumbling away into the trees. But the violet energy broke against the shield like waves on a cliff. Draub's morning star slashed down, missing Mor'kar'kuul by a hair's breadth as Gallarin barged him aside.

The captain rose with his sword in hand. "Stand down, Draub."

"You're a fool, Captain. These savages are responsible for the curse. I probably just saved the royal child—and your own whelp!" Draub indicated the man whose head he had crushed.

"But if what he told us is true..."

"Of course, it isn't true. These people drink deceit from their mothers' teats."

Draub advanced, swinging his morning star. With his shield, Gallarin would have eased the blows aside. With just a sword, he was forced to dodge and parry, each block ringing up his arms. Sensation faded from his fingers. Catching a strike squarely, Gallarin's blade shattered inches above the hilt. He tossed the broken weapon at Draub and, as the inquisitor raised the shield, kicked forward into a roll. He came up under Draub's next swing and smashed the inquisitor to the ground. By the time Draub recovered his breath, Gallarin had a hand around his throat.

"His death will not be necessary."

It was the seated man who spoke and, as Gallarin watched, the blades of grass upon which he lay moved like a surgeon's needle, stitching together his broken flesh. The golden circlet twisted back into its original shape, and he rose gracefully while the final glimmers of green wove themselves into his skin.

"You have the knowledge you need," he told Gallarin. "What you do with it now is up to you."

5

The silence in the throne room told Gallarin that his words had been understood. He bowed low before King Agathenes, and left the royal court to make of it what they would. Princess Zamina was not present but she would hear soon enough. In the courtyard, Gallarin hurried to his horse and leapt into the saddle. Behind him, guards were shouting. He did not wait to see what they were saying.

Jollista was waiting for him at the edge of the city. Her eyes were frightened, and she clutched her swollen belly. He had told her so little, but she had trusted him. He kissed her—fiercely, protectively—lifted her into the saddle and took the reins.

They headed west, into the hills, where shadows presaged the approaching night. Gallarin had chosen this time to speak with the king, for it gave them the best chance of slipping away unseen. What he had told Agathenes challenged *everything*, and Gallarin knew that he would never be allowed to simply leave.

Jollista groaned as Gallarin's horse stumbled on the uneven track.

"I'm fine," she promised him, but he saw the strain on her face. One of her hands gripped the saddle, but the other did not leave the curve of her middle.

There was no warning as figures stepped from behind rocks and barred the way forward. Others appeared, flanking the trail. Gallarin drew his sword and placed himself between the men and his wife.

Inquisitor Draub shouldered his way to the front of the men. His eyes glistened, coldly. "I have orders to arrest you, traitor."

Gallarin lifted his sword, but did not speak.

"I look forward to our time together in the Hall of Questions." Draub's teeth flashed in the gathering gloom. "Your wife, also."

A clutch of men rushed forward to seize Gallarin, but their hands passed through him as if he were shadow. His image rippled like disturbed water and then settled. The men jerked back, fearful and confused.

Draub ran forward, swung his morning star, and almost toppled over when it met no resistance. He tried to seize the horse's reins and glanced at his empty hands. No, not empty. In his palm were grains of sand that glittered in the last rays of the setting sun.

Draub clenched his fists as rage filled him.

On a different hill, almost a mile to the south, Gallarin paused and exchanged a glance with Thestia. They had both heard the echo of Draub's enraged shout.

The mage smiled. "It worked."

Opening the bag at her waist, Thestia waited for the last grains of sand to whip through the air and settle within.

By the time they reached the bottom of the hill, night was all around them.

"Where will you go?" Thestia asked.

Gallarin glanced up at his wife. "Beyond the border. And you?"

"Mor'kar'kuul is determined to free those who are imprisoned. I may help him."

"We thank you," said Jollista. "All three of us."

Entwining her fingers, Thestia touched them to her heart and head.

Gallarin led the horse along the trail into the soft darkness and on towards the frontier.

Meet the Author
Carl Walmsley

Thanks for taking the time to answer a few questions. Start by giving our readers a short bio. Who are you and how long have you been writing?

Carl grew up listening to his mother's tales of fantastic creatures and strange new worlds. He was never quite the same again – and is quite relieved about that. Carl has worked as a teacher, an actor and a writer for various roleplaying games.

Congratulations on placing a story in the pages of Savage Realms. We get inundated with stories every month and only a few are chosen. Is this your first story with Savage Realms? Have you published other stories in previous magazines? If so tell the readers which issue they can find those stories in.

I've written several short stories, including 'Nana' which was published in The Magazine of Fantasy and Science Fiction (March 2022). I've penned a number of tales for Rogue Blades Entertainment, along with The Common Tongue Magazine (issue 4) and Daily Science Fiction.

Tell us a little more about your main character? What motivates them? And what motivates you to write about them?

I have always enjoyed conflicted characters, particularly when they are forced to question their core beliefs and make a decision at the end of the story that they would not have made at the start. Conversely, a good antagonist is sure of themselves and won't change their view. It's this certainty that enables them to terrible things. Gallarin is torn between duty and what he sees with his own eyes. It's that struggle which give him his arc.

Will we be seeing any more of this character in the future?

At the end of this tale, Gallarin has abandoned his home and is heading out into the unknown. Who knows what he might find there?

Being published is a rare thing. Some writers work their whole life and never make it happen. You did. Give other aspiring writers a little advice and hope for the future.

Every time you set pen to paper (or finger to keyboard) it's a chance to learn something new. To start with, that thing can be all about improving your skills (a process that goes on forever!), but you also need clarity about what you want to say. What little bit of experience or understanding do you want to express in your story? Working that out makes the whole thing a lot easier. Oh, and read. A lot.

Finally, what are you reading right now? Is it any good? And what's the one sword and sorcery story every fan should read at least once before they die?

I'm reading Battle Ground – book 17 in The Dresden Files. Jim Butcher rocks, but he really needs to crack on and write book 18. Please! Tales of Fafhrd and the Gray Mouser are well worth seeking out, along with everything written by David Gemmell.

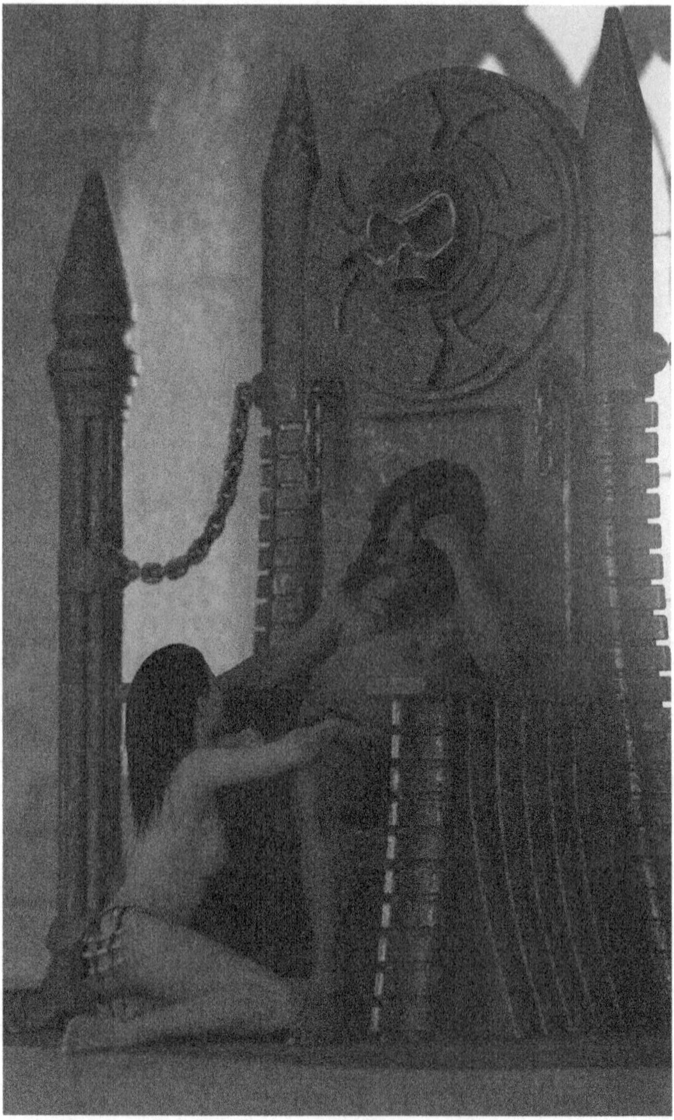

The Voice in the Mist

by Grayson Sullivan

Coals and embers sparkled in the fireplace. The Skops Promise Inn and Tavern was empty except for a group of men huddled about the fireplace, keeping warm and sipping their ale. The Innkeeper leaned on the counter, his head in his hands, trying to rest his eyes before night. His wife stepped away from a cauldron of spicy stew and busied herself sweeping the floor. A collective attitude of exhaustion hung over the room like a blanket over weary shoulders.

The door flew open and a rush of cold air blew into the tavern. Rain drizzled outside and into the tavern stepped a man, soaking wet. He had a mane of thick black hair, although his beard was gray. Braided from the chin, it extended down his barrel chest. He had hunter's eyes and a hooked nose that resembled a falcon's beak. He closed the door and scanned the room. Suspicious eyes greeted him.

The man wiped the raindrops from his leather gambeson and ran his fingers over the fur lining on the collar. He went to the counter, where the weary innkeeper raised his eyes to meet him.

"We cannot welcome visitors as of now," said the Innkeeper. "You have my apologies, stranger."

The innkeeper's wife made her way around the counter and jabbed the innkeeper in the ribs with her broomstick. "But we can make an exception for you."

"Forgive me," said the stranger. "I do not mean to impose. I have been traveling for some time and I have not slept on anything but the hard ground for weeks. I have not slept well at all. If I am not welcome in Burhred..."

"If my wife says you are welcome in Burhred, then you are welcome," said the innkeeper, blinking to stay awake. "For extra coin, I can give you food and drink before bed."

After paying, the stranger received a tankard of ale and a bowl of stew from the innkeeper. The innkeeper looked at the group by the fireplace and leaned in close. "You best be in bed early," he said, "and leave after sunrise."

"I will be gone before sunrise," said the stranger.

"I said after," the innkeeper insisted, knocking his fist on the counter.

The stranger lowered his tankard and grunted. He looked about the room, inspecting the band of men who were whispering to themselves. They stood and made their way to the door, glancing sidelong at the stranger. The door opened, and the sun was setting outside. The last man turned as if he wanted to say something, but held his tongue and closed the door.

The innkeeper's wife eyed the stranger, and she noted that he carried an arming sword on his belt. She blinked in disbelief. Grabbing her husband's attention, she gestured toward the pommel of the sword, which was molded to resemble a bear's head. The Innkeeper's jaw dropped.

"By the powers, you were one of the king's wardens," he said to the stranger, who kept his eyes on his food. "Not that it's a problem. We just haven't seen a warden around since... Well, I say what happened to you wardens was wrong, and the king got what he deserved."

"I will have my room now," the stranger said, changing the subject and scraping the last bit of stew from his bowl.

"Right, but first things first," said the innkeeper. "We keep a log. We need your name for our records."

"Gamel Thorne." The old warden swigged down the last of his ale and followed the innkeeper's wife to a room, rubbing his back and trying to remember the last time he slept. She led with a candle to an upstairs room with a small table, a chair and a bed. Gamel noted that someone had boarded up the window and sealed it with tar.

"What is the reason for this?" He pointed to the window.

The woman's face flushed. She went to the door.

"A broken window. We boarded it up to keep the rain out," she said. "Call if you need anything."

With that, she closed the door.

The keyhole was sealed with tar. Something strange was happening in this tavern. He examined his surroundings and wondered if they might try to murder him in his sleep. Jarring the door with the chair,

Gamel kicked off his boots and made himself ready for bed. He laid down and exhaling, he closed his eyes but kept his sword in his hand.

Somewhere in the night came the sound of weeping. Gamel, who would otherwise be sleeping soundly, turned in his bed. He thought the sound of a child calling for its mother and wondered if anyone was going help the child. The sound was growing more severe, and the old man pulled the pillow over his head.

Outside in the night, the sound of tears became shrieks of pain. They grew so loud that Gamel was once again awake but now alarmed. Surely this village had a watchman or local guard who would investigate? Gamel sat for a moment in the dark, his hand on his sword, ready to act.

The screams turned to an unearthly, garbled voice, which shouted demonic profanities so loudly that it made Gamel's ears ring. Next came a thumping on the walls of the inn as if a man was banging a door. On and on it went, garbled threats and slamming walls, until it struck Gamel that he was sleeping on the second floor and no man could beat on the second-story wall like this. This had all the marks of being wicked and unnatural.

Drawing his blade, Gamel sprang from his bed with the energy of a much younger man. Racing down the darkened hall, down the stairs, and into the tavern, his ears assaulted the whole way by the insane speech. Glancing around the room, he noticed that they had also boarded up the ground-floor windows. He moved toward the door.

Crossing the counter, he noticed the innkeeper and his wife seated on the floor. They held their hands over their ears. Gamel cursed the man for a coward and flung the door open to reveal a thick white mist. Without a second thought, he stepped into the night. The monstrous shouting was now louder than ever. Gamel wandered with his sword held out in front of him, unable to see in the mist.

The shouting came to an abrupt stop. Gamel stood with the mist swirling around him, peering into the thick of it. For a moment, the air was calm, and the world was silent. Then the voice spoke.

"You aren't one of them," it whispered. "You don't belong here."

"Who are you?" Gamel spoke through clenched teeth.

The voice resumed its furious tantrum. Gamel could not stand the sound of it and raised a hand to cover his ear, but paused when he felt something warm and wet trickle down his arm. Blood! The mist had sliced through Gamel's skin. He swung his sword, thrashing at some invisible attacker, but the mist vanished without a trace.

Gamel collapsed, leaning on his sword. He panted for breath, trying to make sense of what he just experienced. Making his way back to the Inn, the owners greeted him at the door. They had pitiful looks on their faces and invited Gamel to come and have his wounds treated.

"It is like this every night," The innkeeper said as his wife washed Gamel's wounds. "For a year now, the mist comes. With it comes that voice, which shrieks evil words and keeps us all awake. It beats on the walls of every building, and anyone caught outside is torn to shreds."

"That's why you board your windows," Gamel asked, "to keep the mist out?"

The innkeeper nodded.

"Do you know where it came from?" Gamel asked.

The innkeeper gave his wife a pensive look and shook his head. "One strange thing," he said. "It has never disappeared like that before. Something about your presence drove it away. I'm going to have to tell the mayor about it. I don't expect he will let you leave until he examines you."

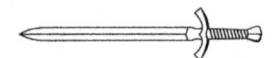

The Mayor was a frail man with wispy white hair, a gaunt face, and missing teeth. Still, he had a commanding presence about him which Gamel could appreciate. He sat on a chair with a high back and wore a velvet robe. Gnarled fingers grasped the armrest. Like all the people in Burhred, he looked exhausted.

The Mayor's house was lavish compared to the rest of the village. A high ceiling and lush carpets. A servant girl placed a cup of hot tea on the table next to the mayor. She turned to leave, and the mayor's eyes followed her, his mouth curving into a lecherous grin. The mayor's personal guard leaned on their pikes, doing their best to seem formidable instead of weary.

"We have welcomed a warden into our humble village," said the mayor. "One of the king's own taskforce. Investigating treason and serving as judge and executioner. At least you did before the king was overthrown. Tell me, warden, what brought you to Burhred?"

Gamel looked at the mayor with contempt. In days gone by, he would have disemboweled him for such candid talk. "I was traveling by the river. The road led me to your village, where I stopped to rest."

"And did you rest well?" asked the Mayor.

Gamel let out a sigh. "You know I did not."

"No, you did not," the mayor responded. "None of us have for a year. Those of us who survived the mist, that is."

Gamel started, but the mayor raised his hand to silence him. "My name is Alnod. I have been the mayor here for twenty-five years. In all this time, we were a peaceful and prosperous village. One year ago, the mist appeared. It came without warning during a festival, and slaughtered a good number of innocent townsfolk. Now we try to sleep during the day and barricade ourselves at night. It has caused our economy to suffer."

"Why don't you lead these people to a safe place?" Gamel asked.

"And leave Burhred? By the powers, are you mad?" he asked. "It is not so easy to leave your ancestral home as it is for wardens to wander."

"And why don't you let me wander?" asked Gamel, impatience in his voice.

"Because the mist fled after it attacked you. It seems to fear you, or perhaps it submits to some magic you wield?"

"I wield no magic. Wardens are not sorcerers," Gamel responded.

"In any case, I think you are of use to us," Mayor Alnod said. "If you track down the source of this mist, I can offer you a reward. You can have your pick of my treasury."

Gamel did not need money, but he ran his thumb over the pommel of his sword, remembering the old days when he hunted sorcerers and uncovered the secret meeting rooms of revolutionaries. His heart beat with excitement, recalling times of adventure, danger, and rogue warfare.

"Tonight, Alnod, Mayor of Burhred, I will find the source of this mist. I will endeavor to break its power, or die trying."

The sun was sinking fast. Warm golden beams shot through the clouds, betraying the cold bite of the wind. Gamel had taken a position on a hill overlooking Burhred. It would only be a matter of time before sunset, and he would see which direction the mist would blow in from. Gamel laid back on the grass, still wet from the night before. A pain cappered down his back and he briefly wondered if he was too old for this type of work. Then his thoughts returned to the task at hand.

In all his years as a warden, Gamel had developed a nose for sniffing out lies, and no one in town had been completely truthful. Still, the uncanny mist was clearly an act of sorcery or some evil creature. Gamel hated lies, but he hated sorcery even more.

Darkness fell. The eyes of the old warden watched as people hurried into their homes. For a moment, nothing happened. Then, from the woods opposite the hill where he lay, Gamel watched a thick white mist slither like a serpent out of the trees, over the grass, and into the village. It spread between the buildings. Gamel listened for the voice in the mist, as he made his way around the town toward the distant woods.

The moon cast long, creeping shadows among the trees, but Gamel kept a steady pace, heedless of roots that might trip him or low hanging branches. He walked all night among the trees. Hours had passed and he finally noticed a pale light in the east. Dawn was fast approaching, but he'd found no clue to the origin of the mist.

Gamel stopped a moment to find his bearings, and when he did, a foul odor filled his nostrils. The stench of death. He examined his surroundings, and to his horror, spied a small child. A boy, no older than seven, laying dead against a tree. Gamel stepped close. The rancid smell was coming from the boy. His eyes were open, but they were cloudy and translucent. His skin was cold and clammy to the touch, and his complexion pale, like all his blood was missing.

Gamel examined the area. Murder? There were no visible wounds on the child. The old warden circled the corpse, curious. As he rounded the body, he heard shrieking and garbled, demonic speech. He turned to see the mist rushing toward him with incomprehensible speed. before he could so much as move, it flew past him and up the dead child's nose. The boy's eyes gave a sudden movement, and he sprang to his feet as if he had only been sleeping. He still stank of death , but now he moved.

"You don't belong here," the voice shouted. It was coming from the boy but his lips never moved.

Gamel drew his sword and lept to the attack. He cut through flesh and bone. Yet the thing merely stared at him, dead eyes set. The wounds disappeared. A tickle of fear crept up Gamel's neck.

The monster threw himself hard at Gamel. He swatted with open palms, possessing the strength of five men in each arm. Gamel flew backward and landed on a great dirty root. His body was searing with pain, and he let out a strangled cry. Jumping back to his feet, he glared at the creature. He charged again, this time dodging the creature's attack and slamming his sword's crossguard into its forehead, leaving a dent and sending it to the ground.

Gamel raised his blade to decapitate the evil creature, when it spoke.

"Wait," it said without moving its mouth. "My fight is not with you. You are not one of them."

"What is this?" Gamel responded. "A monster begging for mercy when it has offered none?"

"I do not need mercy. I cannot die by the sword." it said. "Mayor Alnod saw to that."

Gamel lowered his blade, confused. "This is devilry. If the sword cannot kill you, then what can? Tell me, and I will end your life."

"My life will end with the villagers," he said.

Gamel said, "I have never met a devil or sorcerer that couldn't die by the sword. And you speak of Alnod? What of him?"

"He did this to me," the boy said. "The villagers too. I am bound to their lives, so I cannot die until they do."

Gamel stood over the corpse, staring in disbelief.

"Do not deceive me," Gamel said. "You have been tormenting that village for a year, shrieking and pounding on the walls of the buildings. You keep them awake, and when they wander outside, you cut them to pieces, just as you did with me."

"Let me tell you the truth," the corpse boy said.

Gamel took a breath and looked at the cuts on his arms. "You attacked me," he said. "why?"

"I did not wish for you to stay in the village," the corpse boy said. "I had hoped you would leave, but here you are hunting me like a beast."

After watching the thing for a moment, Gamel sheathed his sword. "Do you have a name?"

The thing thought for a moment. Its hollow eyes moved back and forth in thought. "Yes, I think so," he said. "Sometimes I don't remember all, but I know my name. I am Ivo. That's what my mother called me. That's where my story begins. With my mother."

"Tell me," Gamel said. "But do not lie to me. If a blade can't kill you, I will find something that can."

Ivo nodded in understanding. "I lived in Burhred with my mother. My father died two years ago. He was a good man. They found his body hung up in the trees in this very forest. Some thought a wild beast had killed him, others spoke of sorcery. My mother carried on with me, taking good care of me. She was a baker, so we always had enough to eat.

"One day, while Mother was buying flour in the market, I wandered away to see the tax collector's new horse. It was beautiful, and I wanted to pet it. When I got too close, it reared back and kicked me in my head. The last thing I remember is my mother crying and the village folk gathered around me. I remember waking up days later in my bed. My mother was happy, and she took me in her arms and danced across the room with me. I had been dead, but I was alive again."

"Sorcery," spat Gamel. "The foulest kind. No man is meant to tamper with the dead. This is necromancy."

"I never knew what to call it," Ivo said. "I only knew that I was alive again. After some time, I realized that something was wrong. People avoided me in the streets. Some treated me like I was dangerous, and others complained about how I smelled. Mother did all she could to make it better, covering me in perfumes and spices. Then I would go to bed at night and have dreams where I traveled about the village. I went all over and found that I could squeeze through keyholes and open windows. I came to realize that this was not a dream, that I never sleep, and that I could become like mist in the nighttime."

Gamel listened with a hand on the hilt of his sword. He stroked his beard, occasionally nodding, but not convinced of the boy's story.

"I remember the day they came for my mother," Ivo said. "She was accused of witchcraft by Mayor Alnod. The entire village was outside of our house. The mayor put Mother on trial and the entire village turned on her. They kept her in jail for a long time, but I would come and visit her in the night. I tried to comfort her, but she only cried. One day the Guards came for her. They drug her into the streets and forced me to watch as they tied her between two horses. They cursed at her, throwing rotten food at her. Then they gave the horses a command to run, and the horses tore her in half."

Gamel squeezed his eyes shut.

"The villagers turned on me. They ran me out of the village and sent me away," Ivo continued. "I was alone and angry. I did not understand why they did that to my mother. In my anger, I realized I could hurt people, that I was strong and nobody could hurt me. But I am strongest at night. That is why I torment Burhred. Do you understand now?"

"If what you say is true, then yes, I understand," said Gamel. "But what role does Alnod play?"

"He practices sorcery in secret. He uses it to possess men to carry out his wicked deeds. He confuses young girls and takes advantage of them and visits any who openly speak out against him with strange dooms. My mother knew he was a sorcerer, and visited him in secret, begging him to bring me back to life. He agreed, on the condition that she offer him her body.

"My mother was a good woman, beautiful and kind, but she was desperate. She gave herself to the old man, and he kept his word. What he did not tell her was that I would not be as I was. That I would be a monster, and that the cost of unnatural resurrection was to borrow life from everyone in the village. I am bound to their lives, and I cannot die until every single one of them does."

"Alnod betrayed your mother by accusing her of witchcraft?" Gamel asked. "Do you offer any proof of this, or am I meant to take you at your word?"

"The proof has been sneaking up on you. Look!"

Gamel turned. Five of Alnod's guards were bearing down on him, pikes lowered. They meant to skewer him, but the old warden was too sharp and too well-trained. He drew his sword and drove himself between the pikes. He ran his blade through one man and turned to engage the rest. Two men attacked Ivo. The other two set their eyes on Gamel.

The battle raged. Ivo was tossed men with sweeps of his hands and Gamel wielded his blade as only a warden could. He parried to the left and right, avoiding his enemy's pikes, and narrowly missing their throats with his sword. The guards drew their swords when Gamel positioned himself among a patch of small trees, rendering the pikes useless. Now, in close quarters, Gamel was in his element.

He unleashed one blow after another. He deflected a weak strike and brought his sword down on the guard's helmet so hard that sparks flew and the man fell unconscious to the ground. The other guard tried to disarm Gamel but found himself open to an iron fist that closed on his throat. Gamel took a breath as his enemy struggled to break free then struck a killing blow.

Ivo had mangled one guard with brute strength. Only a single guard remained. Realizing that he was going to die, he dropped his pike and ran. Gamel picked up the abandoned pike, took aim, and threw. The weapon pinned the man to a tree. Gamel approached him and jerked the pike free, letting the body to fall to the ground.

The boy stood still as if nothing had happened. Gamel breathed heavily, trying to steady himself as he retrieved his sword. He inspected his surroundings, checking for more attackers. After a moment he turned to Ivo.

"Your power is greatest at night?" Gamel wiped the blood from his blade. "You seem rather unstoppable right now."

"Will you help me?" Ivo asked. "Will you help me bring the village of Burhred to account?"

Gamel took a breath, the foul smell of the boy filling his nose. Taking a seat on a fallen log, he looked at the boy. Alnod had at the very least betrayed him. The mayor must have spent a year looking for the boy and may have suspected that Gamel would hear his story. He took a moment to consider the facts and knew in his heart that it was the truth.

Gamel stood, stretched his arms and rubbed his aching back. Only just now did he realize how tired he was. Gamel had spent the entire evening prowling the woods, and now it was morning. He nodded. "Yes, boy. I will help you," he said. "And tonight, after you have found your justice, I hope you find your death, you miserable thing."

Ivo merely stared at him, his dead eyes forming what looked like tears. "I will die when they do."

"Then let's be on with it," Said Gamel. "The way is long, and I have much to prepare."

Alnod lay in his posh bed sleeping soundly. This was the first time the mist had not come for a year, and he relished the moment. He dreamed perverse dreams. Some part of his mind came to consciousness, as he smiled and laughed to himself in his sleep, believing his wicked schemes had worked. His guards had no doubt found Gamel and the corpse boy, and would return soon with news of their deaths.

His joy came to a halt when he smelled smoke. Rising with alarm, he saw his roof in flames. He shouted in fear as he fled from his sheets and down the stairs. He burst through the front door to find that the entire village was on fire, and the people were fleeing their homes.

"Where is the fire brigade?" Alnod demanded. No one answered him. Each man was looking after his own interest. Alnod made his way to the village square, where a great gathering had circled around something or someone. Pushing his way to the center, he found the king's warden. Gamel stood with his hunter's eyes fixed on Alnod, and in his hand was a cloth bag stuffed with something heavy.

"Alnod, Mayor of Burhred!" Gamel shouted. "I found the source of your cursed mist."

All eyes turned to Alnod, who stood in his night clothes and took in the sight. "I knew you would, but we have more pressing matters now. Help us fight the fires!"

Gamel emptied his bag and sent five heads rolling to the feet of Alnod. The villagers gasped and cried, and old Alnod let out a squeal like a pig.

"There is your source," Gamel said, pointing at Alnod. "You are responsible."

"He started the fires! He killed the guards! Kill him!" Alnod jabbed a finger at Gamel.

The crowd fell on Gamel, tearing at his leather gambeson and scratching at his head. They pulled and shoved, kicked and punched, and Gamel took a beating. Shouts of spite and hatred floated through the air. Gamel only laughed.

The mist had encircled the village. It loomed tall like a wall and imposed itself on the villagers. The light of the fires cast shadows on the white wall of the mist, shadows that danced and mocked like heathens around a campfire. A hush fell over the crowd.

"A year ago you made a deal, Alnod," Gamel declared. "You used sorcery to raise a boy from the dead for a widow's embrace. You have been using sorcery to do many evils in this village, including clouding the memory of the young women you prey on."

"Lies," cried Alnod. "Lies! Silence these lies!"

"That is how you remained in power," continued the warden. "You cast spells and enchantments to control people, and even used your sorcery to kill innocent men. Your lust raged so fiercely that you made a deal to raise a boy from the dead. But just as you demanded a price, the sorcery demanded a price. A price you gladly paid, for you have traded the lives of all of Burhred for a night of passion."

The crowd murmured.

Alnod clenched gnarled fists.

"Is it not true that you drove a boy from the village?" shouted Gamel. "A foul-smelling boy whose mother someone had accused of witchcraft?"

"That's true," Shouted a man. "We exiled an unnatural child."

"And did you not force him to watch as you executed his mother for witchcraft?" Gamel asked. "An innocent woman, accused of witchcraft by Alnod, and only by Alnod?"

"There were no other accusers. What if this is the truth?" came a voice.

"Search the mayor's house," cried another. "Look for evidence of sorcery."

Men ran into Alnod's burning house, racing against time, seeking proof that he was secretly a sorcerer. The mist continued to build, encircling the village, while a handful of daring villagers attempted to flee and found themselves mercilessly slaughtered.

Alnod nervously rubbed his palms together. He grabbed one man by the collar and tried to mutter some defense, but the man pushed him away. Alnod gave a chilling glare at Gamel.

"This man made a sorcerer's oath to raise a boy from the dead, and he bound you all to his fate," cried Gamel. "You all took part in the murder of an innocent woman, and you all must stand to account."

No sooner did Gamel speak these words than the group of men emerged from Alnod's house. "We saw it. Beneath the main floor of his home, a workshop. There were books and strange crystals. A mirror for spying on people through some supernatural power and an altar with the blood of animals. We found his journal, and he confesses all. He signed our lives away with his magic, and he led us to murder Ivo's mother."

Alnod let out a great shriek, and raising his hands in the air, he sent out a shockwave that knocked the crowd of villagers to their backs. He pointed a single gnarled finger at Gamel, shouting profanities and curses. The crowd raised themselves to their feet and rushed Alnod, lifting him above their heads and walking him to the village stocks.

"Burn him!"

Alnod only laughed. He mocked and taunted the crowd as they raged at him. The fires roared all about them, sending smoke billowing into the sky. Gamel looked on with disgust. He had seen many strange things as a warden, but this was the strangest sight of all. A man from the crowd produced a flaming piece of debris, and with it, he set fire to Alnod.

At first, he only screamed, but soon the screams became demented laughter. After the fire had burned away his flesh, his skeleton remained. It moved and laughed, and muttered curses. The villagers were terrified. They had never dreamed that such a man would be in their midst. Now, everyone saw the man for what he was.

Alnod's skeleton continued to cackle until the fire devoured his bones. Finally, his bones fell apart and burst into dust. The stunned villagers watched in shock. Before long, a great cry broke out among the crowd. The villagers looked around them at the mist, which floated just beyond the fire.

Gamel found his way to the well. He drew up a bucket of water and took a drink. He felt a hand on his shoulder. It was the innkeeper.

"Can you do nothing to help us, warden?" he asked. "Take pity on us."

"You dare ask for pity?" Gamel said. "You took my money and put my life at risk. How many other travelers suffered? How many died, or were scared beyond life itself, because you hid the truth? Besides, Alnod sealed your fate. There is nothing I can do."

"Please," The innkeeper wept. "Aren't wardens supposed to be for the people?"

"What did you do? The day the boy's mother was murdered?" asked Gamel.

The innkeeper stared at him. "I lent them my horse," he said, through tears. "I helped them kill her."

Gamel shook his head in disdain. "Wardens believe in the law," he said. "This place is lawless."

After filling his flagon with water, Gamel rummaged through some barrels in the market, retrieving a satchel of fruit. He made his way through the crowd of condemned people and stepped up to the edge of the mist. He took a breath and stepped in, making his way to the other side without a scratch. So began Gamel's journey out of Burhred.

Making his way down the road, Gamel rubbed at his shoulder, and then his back. He pulled an apple from the satchel. How long had it been since he had eaten? The tavern two nights ago. He crested the hill that overlooks Burhred and heard the screams.

"It shouldn't be this hard," he said, "to find a good night's sleep."

Meet the Author
Grayson Sullivan

Thanks for taking the time to answer a few questions. Start by giving our readers a short bio. Who are you and how long have you been writing?

I am Grayson D Sullivan, a Texan by birth, Arkansan by circumstance, and married to the love of my life. We enjoy camping, movies, music, and good books, and expect our first child very soon. I have been writing since 2022 after my wife encouraged me to take all my crazy ideas and put them down on paper.

Congratulations on placing a story in the pages of Savage Realms. We get inundated with stories every month and only a few are chosen. Is this your first story with Savage Realms? Have you published other stories in previous magazines? If so tell the readers which issue they can find those stories in.

I am honored to say that this is my first story with Savage Realms, or any magazines at all, for that matter. I just self-published a novella, and you can find numerous stories posted on my substack if you would like to read more of my work.

Tell us a little more about your main character? What motivates them? And what motivates you to write about them?

I wanted to write an aging character. Someone whose best years are behind them, who grew up in a world that no longer exists. Gamel is still driven by the moral compass instilled in him in his youth, a leftover from a more structured world. I am approaching forty, and as I watch the world transform around me, I suppose I relate very much to Gamel, who doesn't exactly recognize the world he occupies. Growing older gives me all the more reason to cling to the values I was taught as a young man.

Will we be seeing any more of this character in the future?

I have numerous stories that feature Gamel floating around my hard drive. I also have an unpublished novel set about twenty years prior that explains what happened to the king and the wardens. Someday, I will have that published.

Being published is a rare thing. Some writers work their whole life and never make it happen. You did. Give other aspiring writers a little advice and hope for the future.

I am of the pulp writer's mindset. If you want to write, then you need to stop wanting and start doing. Write, don't wait for inspiration. Ideas are everywhere; grab one and apply the storytelling components—action, character, conflict, pacing, etc. Study the genre you write in and lose yourself in your story. Take the tale seriously, but don't take yourself too seriously. Read the kinds of stories you want to write and set yourself loose.

Finally, what are you reading right now? Is it any good? And what's the one sword and sorcery story every fan should read at least once before they die?

I read across multiple genres. The story I am reading is Merona Grant and the Lost Tomb of Golgotha. It is a love letter to Indiana Jones and the Mummy, featuring a female protagonist like Tomb Raider. I am enjoying it immensely. As for the one sword and sorcery story, every fan should read, how could I answer with anything other than The Tower of the Elephant by Robert E. Howard? For my money, it encompasses everything great about sword and sorcery and is among the best written.

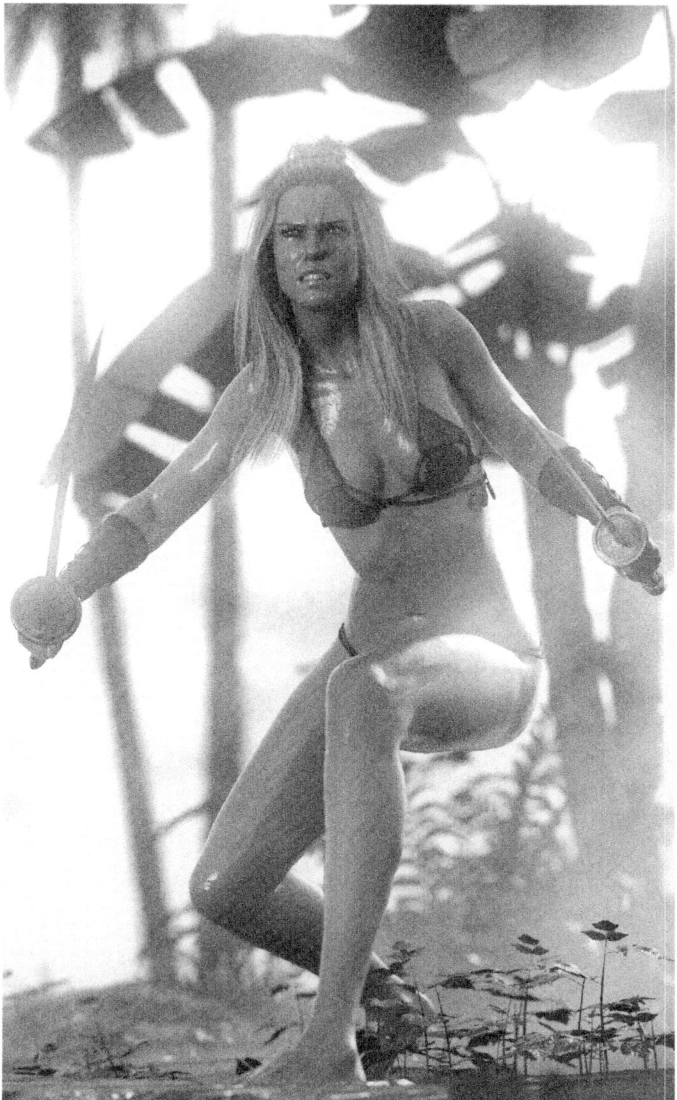

Free Book Offer

Get a FREE Novel

Need more sword swinging action? Grab a FREE copy of Willard Black's phenomenal fantasy adventure novel THE SAVAGE REALMS. It's our gift to you, absolutely free!

SAVAGE REALMS MONTHLY: MARCH 2025

Click HERE to start reading today!

Interested in advertising with us?

Have you published a fantasy or science fiction book? Are you struggling to get sales? Would you'd like to reach potentially thousands of new readers?

Place an advertisement with Savage Realms Monthly!

We've got a dedicated fan base eager to find new and exciting books by talented authors.

Reach out to us: https://www.literaryrebel.com/contact/ to discuss ad options.

Submissions

Submissions

Are you a sword and sorcery fan? Do you pen tales of savages and wizards in your spare time? Have you always wanted to be a published author, but don't know where to start? Literary Rebel is seeking talented authors to feature in Savage Realms Monthly! The best part... We pay!

Send us your best sword and sorcery themed tale of no more than ten thousand (10,000) words and, if we like it, we'll pay for first publishing rights. Don't worry, you as the author will retain the copyright to all characters and locales so you are free to publish stories within your fictional universe in other publications in the future. We'll even link to any websites, social media, or storefronts you desire.

http://savagerealmsmonthly.com/submissions/

Afterword

Afterword

Did we slake your thirst for brawny barbarians, evil wizards, and lusty wenches? We certainly hope so. If you enjoyed this issue, please let us know by leaving a review on Amazon. Reviews help other like-minded readers discover Savage Realms Monthly and puts coin in the coffers so we can pay future talent. The best part is, it doesn't cost you a copper penny.

We want to sincerely thank you for picking up Savage Realms Monthly and we promise we'll be back next month with another exciting crop of axe wielding barbarians for your reading pleasure.

If you want to be notified of upcoming issues, follow the magic runes: https://dl.bookfunnel.com/jozt5ktaub to be added to our mailing list. We'll let you know when the next issue hits the stands. And we promise no spam. Ever.

Until next time, keep your swords sharp!

CARL WALMSEY, TIM GERSTMAR, GRAYSON SULLIVAN

INTRODUCING THE GRINDHOUSE A CONAN EXILES SERVER

HOSTED BY SAVAGE REALMS MONTHLY

COLLECT ALL YOUR FAVORITE ISSUES

Miss an issue? Grab all your favorite sword and sorcery fiction: bit.ly/SavageMag

Printed in Great Britain
by Amazon